MANDI'S LITTLE MOTHER'S DAY
A HOLIDAYS AT RAWHIDE RANCH STORY

ELLIE ROSE

This is a work of fiction. Names, characters, businesses, places, events, and incidents are either the products of the author's imagination or used in a fictitious manner. Any resemblance to actual persons, living or dead, or actual events is purely coincidental.

No part of the book may be reproduced or transmitted in any form or by any means, electronic or mechanical, including photocopying, recording, or by any information storage and retrieval system, without permission in writing from the publisher.

2024 © Published by A and A Publications. All rights reserved.

Holidays at Rawhide Ranch

Mandi's Little Mothers' Day

Edited by Maggie Ryan

Cover by AllyCat's Creations

This book is intended for adults only. Spanking and other sexual activities represented in this book are fantasies only, intended for adults. Nothing in this book should be interpreted as the author's advocating any non-consensual spanking/sexual activity or the spanking of minors.

For more Rawhide Ranch stories check out this link - https://linktr.ee/Rawhide

DEDICATION

This one's for me. Heal, little one, it will be okay.

AUTHOR NOTE

Please be aware that this story contains autistic meltdowns, references to anxiety, C-PTSD and an (off-page) abusive alcoholic ex. I hope I have treated Mandi's experiences and emotions with the care that she and you deserve.

CHAPTER 1

Mandi barely looked up as the cab passed through the gates of Rawhide Ranch. It had been so long since she'd been outside of her tiny duplex that even the idea of swapping one room for another on a ranch felt overwhelming. She clutched her bear to her, fiddling with the glasses that perched atop his nose.

She'd gone to her cousin Ralphie's workplace the previous week, to get Beau's glasses mended, and Ralphie had taken one look at her, demanded that his fiancé Nate drop everything to take over for him, and had whisked her off to lunch.

That had made her nervous; Ralphie was sweet but vivacious. Startlingly so.

But he hadn't been loud or overwhelming. Her cousin had been kind and quiet, and when he'd mended Beau's glasses for her, he'd told her that Rawhide Ranch would mend her too, if she let it.

Mandi wasn't sure what he meant by that—not the broken bit, she knew she was broken—but what he thought a ranch could do to fix her, when she couldn't fix herself.

It wasn't like she had many other options though. The indie bookshop she'd been working in was closing, and she was going to need to find something new to do anyway, and Ralphie had almost insisted that she check out this place first.

"It's perfect for you, Mandi," he'd said, his obvious enthusiasm shining through. "The people are the loveliest —although some of them are addicted to pranks—and they also have a library." He'd looked at her slyly then; everyone in their family knew how much she liked books. "They actually have *two* libraries."

"I'm not *that* obsessed with books."

There had been a pause.

"Okay, maybe I am, but that wouldn't be a good enough reason to get me to stay somewhere."

But when he'd brought up their website and showed her all the information, she'd seen one phrase that made her determined to visit Rawhide Ranch: the Littles' Wing.

She clutched Beau more tightly to her as the car came to a stop. A man opened the door to her car, and helped her out, smiling at her. She nodded back quietly, and then looked out to where she was going to stay. The porch stretched the entire length of the very large building in front of her and Mandi could see men and women sitting in basket chairs, rockers and swings, all chattering away, enjoying the May sunshine.

They looked happy.

That bode well. Right?

"You gonna pay or what?" The cab driver's voice was loud and harsh and she flushed and fumbled with her bag, trying to get her purse out quickly. Beau stuffed tightly under one arm, she stuttered sorries and hoped desperately that the people on the porch hadn't heard.

No such luck. A brunette woman came bounding down the steps and over to them. "Is everything okay?"

Mandi's words dried in her mouth, even as she tried to answer, but the cab driver spoke over her. "Yeah, I can't just be sitting idling in my car here. She needs to pay up. Now!"

The last word was even louder and made Mandi jump so much that she dropped her purse altogether.

The brunette skewed him with a look that seemed completely at odds with the pretty, summery dress she wore. "A few moments won't make much of a difference." She turned to the other man and her hands moved in the fluid motions of ASL. His face hardened, and he strode toward the big building.

Then she turned to Mandi, and gently picked up her purse for her. "Hi, I'm Sadie Hawkins. Do you want to give me your card and I'll tap the payment for you?"

Mandi nodded, her eyes darting everywhere but the other woman's face, and silently pulled her card from the open purse that Sadie offered her. Her hands trembled and she held it out, and she was oh so grateful that Sadie didn't say a single thing about how much she was shaking.

"There you go, all paid." Her eyes flashed at the driver, and Mandi impetuously reached out and grabbed her hand, pulling the other woman back toward her and shaking her head ever so slightly. Sadie looked surprised, but followed, and then beamed when a man dressed exactly how Mandi imagined a cowboy would look strode over and rapped smartly on the window of the cab.

"A word, please, driver." His voice was quiet but there was an undercurrent of steel that Mandi flinched at. "Sadie, can you take Ms. Travers through to my office please? Maybe keep her company until I've finished here?"

Sadie slipped her arm into Mandi's and tugged her away from the car. "Now don't you worry, my husband will sort that meanie out and make no mistake. He shouldn't have spoken to you like that!"

In a slight daze, Mandi allowed herself to be led along until she found herself in an overwhelmingly large room, and if it hadn't been for the floor-to-ceiling bookshelves, she'd almost certainly have burst into tears. But instead there were shelves and shelves and shelves of books, all non-fiction, and all organized by subject. She ran her fingers along their spines and allowed herself the smallest of toe wiggles.

When she was truly happy, and felt truly safe, she allowed herself full body wiggles, but she hadn't felt that way for a long time. She hadn't, if she was being truthful with herself, felt safe enough anywhere aside from her duplex for a toe wiggle.

"Is this one of the libraries?" she asked over the shoulder to Sadie. "My cousin said that there were two libraries." Mandi couldn't keep the excitement out of her voice. So many books. And books were safe. Books meant more toe wiggles.

"This? Oh no," said Sadie, "this is my husband's office. There's a library in the Littles' Wing, and another in the University. These are just all his books on law and tax and other boring things."

"Boring? Well now, angel," said Sadie's husband from where he stood in the doorway, "I need boring books to help me run the Ranch."

"You need boring books and me to run the Ranch, Daddy," said Sadie, and went up on tiptoes to kiss his cheek.

"Ms. Travers," he said, turning to Mandi, "Derek Hawkins, but most of the folks round here call me Master Derek. I cannot apologize enough for the interaction you had with your cab driver. We had words and I'm sure he won't be speaking like that to people again."

She nodded her thanks, suddenly shy again, and when he gestured toward one of the large leather chairs, she paused and looked longingly toward the couch in the corner.

"Would you like to sit there, little lady?"

She nodded, still silent, and waited until he smiled before going and tucking herself right up in the corner by the arm of the couch.

Master Derek paused, looking thoughtful, and then walked through the French doors behind his desk, and returned carrying a chair. "I don't want to loom over you," he said.

Mandi was grateful for that. Being loomed over wasn't fun. She didn't like it at all.

"Off you go to class, Sadie," he said, smiling at his wife, but Sadie didn't move, not even when he raised an eyebrow.

"I… would you like me to stay?" The playfulness that had been in her voice earlier was gone now, and she addressed her question to Mandi, not Master Derek.

Mandi nodded, and Sadie looked at her husband. Some unspoken communication passed between them, and then Master Derek inclined his head toward the couch.

Sadie bounced over, her previous seriousness all gone, and clambered up next to Mandi. "Who's this then?"

Mandi was aware of Master Derek leaning back a bit, assessing her, but she tried not to let his scrutiny unsettle her too much. "This is Beau, he's my bear. My cousin mended his glasses because he works at Stuffie Hospital." She looked cautiously toward Master Derek. "Ralphie's the one who suggested I come and stay here. I said so in my emails."

"I remember," he said kindly, so kindly that she felt a little emboldened.

"I get nervous," she said. "But I do want to stay here. It's just that it's all a teensy bit scary really. I am a"—she swallowed—"a Little, I promise, only I think I lost her."

"Lost who?"

"My Little." Mandi had that tight, sick feeling she felt every time she thought about being Little. She clung on to Beau and stroked his fur between her fingers, and rocked back and forth, trying to self-soothe. "I lost my Little because I messed up, and now I can't find her."

CHAPTER 2

"You lost your Little?" Sadie looked horrified. "That sounds awful!" And she hugged Mandi, and Mandi, who—aside from Ralphie—hadn't had any hugs in months, froze.

Sadie noticed and went to move back, but then Mandi buried her face in the other woman's shoulder and held on.

"It's okay," Sadie said, "I'm a Little and there are lots of Littles here, and we'll help you find your Little. We can do a Little hunt for her!"

"Perhaps," Master Derek interjected, "you could explain some more about what you meant by you 'messed up'."

Mandi tried to disentangle herself from Sadie, who wouldn't let her. There was some tussling, and a little bit of giggling, until Sadie eventually let her sit back, as long as Mandi let Sadie hold her hand instead.

She looked at Master Derek, and then immediately looked down. "It's… it's a bit embarrassing."

"That's okay, little lady," he said.

Mandi hadn't really told anyone about it before, so she paused for a few minutes, working out where to start. "I've only really had a Daddy before, and not a Mommy, even though I'm bisexual," she explained, and looked into blue eyes that were warmer than she could have expected. "So just one Daddy. And at first he was funny, and kind, and made me laugh a lot. But it turns out that some Daddies drink too much, and when they do they"—she paused and looked anxiously at them–"Oh! I forgot to give you trigger warnings in case I say something that could be upsetting for you! It's nothing physically bad, not really, but bad words. And he hurt me, emotionally."

Master Derek looked at Sadie, who squeezed Mandi's hand. "Keep going, I'm okay."

"Okay." Mandi took a big deep breath. This next bit was hard. "He wasn't very nice to me sometimes. He said that reading stories to me was weird, because he could feel my Big side waiting to correct him, but I never did! I never even wanted to! I just loved books so much and he wouldn't read to me because I wasn't good enough at being a Little."

She could feel Sadie wanting to say something, but she kept going because if she stopped now, she didn't know if she'd be able to gather up the courage to say it again. "And he said that I was Too Much." Even repeating the words felt like a stab through her heart. "I know that I'm too much sometimes, I do. I can't help it because I'm autistic—as I said in my application—and sometimes sensory things are a bit overwhelming, and I wiggle and make funny noises when I'm happy. But I promise I'll try really hard not to be weird like that while I'm here. I promise."

When she met Master Derek's eyes this time, he looked so sad that she didn't know what to do.

"And then he broke up with me, and I know it was for the best, really, because he wasn't always very nice to me, and I didn't like it when he was drunk and one time when he was drunk…" Something salty touched her lips and Mandi realized that she was crying. "We played and he was so drunk he didn't hear me when I safeworded and I think that's why my Little won't come back! She doesn't trust me to keep her safe anymore."

And with that she buried her face in Beau's fur and sobbed and sobbed. It had felt like a storm, a torrent of words flying hurricane-like out of her mouth, and now that the storm had died down, all that was left in its wake was destruction.

Her.

Destroyed.

She felt a pair of arms draw her close, and then another join them, and for a few minutes she allowed Derek and Sadie Hawkins to hold her, and she felt somewhat safe.

When they pulled back, Sadie was also wiping her eyes.

"Oh, I'm sorry, Sadie," she said, patting her shoulder, "I didn't mean to—"

"You have *nothing* to apologize for," said Sadie fiercely. "Nothing. And we *will* find your Little. I have determined it."

"I agree with my wife," said Master Derek, "We will definitely help you find your Little side again, but you need to know, Mandi, that you didn't mess up. You had a Daddy who didn't look after you the way you deserve to be looked after, but that wasn't your fault. That was all on him."

She knew what he was saying sounded right, but it didn't *feel* right.

"And you will be as weird as you like while you are here. In fact, that may be an order."

A tiny giggle escaped from her.

"And I want to get to know all of your happy noises and wiggles," added Sadie. "Maybe I'll teach you a few noises of my own."

Master Derek looked at her and she subsided into giggles. "But I think perhaps that we might need to slightly alter the Ranch contract for you, Mandi."

She lapsed back into quiet again, having used up all her words and giggles, but she nodded and smiled weakly.

"Most of the rules I'm not too worried about—no drugs, no drinking for Littles and no cussing—but if Littles or guests are naughty, then they're usually subject to punishment, but I don't know"—he looked up and saw Mandi's face—"I think perhaps no corporal punishments for you. And maybe we select one person to take you under their wing, to look after you."

"I'm not looking for a Caregiver," Mandi said, her words quiet but firm. "I don't need a Daddy or a Mommy messing me up again."

"Being a solo Little is a lovely thing for those who want it," said Master Derek, "but not all Daddies or Mommies are bad. Some of them can be just what we need."

She felt her face screw up slightly, and she knew she was going to be stubborn about it when Sadie interjected suddenly. "Oh! Daddy! Mandi loves books and Miss Grayson would be perfect!"

"I don't want—"

"Not like *that*," reassured Sadie, although she did look thoughtful, "she's the librarian in the Littles' Library, and she's been looking for someone to help out for a while. And you did say that you like books!"

Mandi's eyes widened, all thoughts of stubbornness forgotten. "Oh could I?" She turned to Master Derek, suddenly animated. "I promise I'll be good if I can help with the books! The bookstore where I work is closing and I'm so sad about it, but books make me so, so happy."

He laughed. "Okay, little lady. Let me speak to Miss Grayson and see what she thinks. You're booked in to stay with us for a week, yes?"

She nodded. "My job has finished and Ralphie insisted I take a proper holiday for once."

"Well, while you're here, I'm going to insist that you see

one of our counselors, Catherine Denten. I think you'll like her. It's really important that you take care of your mental health, Mandi, so it's going to have to be a condition of your stay."

"Okay," Mandi said quietly. "I can do that I think."

"I'd like you to sit with Sadie and go over the form you filled out before, to double check that it's exactly what you want before you sign it. Afterward, Sadie can take you up to the Guest Wing to get you settled in your room before I bring Miss Grayson to meet you."

Mandi had no intention of finding herself a Mommy or a Daddy while at Rawhide Ranch, but there was something about the name Miss Grayson that sent butterflies fluttering through her stomach. Something that made her wonder whether she was quite so against the idea of a Caregiver after all.

CHAPTER 3

"She's really very, very sweet, Amelia, but absolutely scared of her own shadow, and with good reason, if what she's told us is anything to go by."

Amelia Grayson raised her eyebrows. "What did she tell you?"

Derek leaned back in his chair and sighed. "I'm not going to break her confidence, but she had a faux-Daddy before. The kind who didn't look after her right and has left her hurt and scared and"—he leaned forward to meet her eyes—"she's lost her Little, Amelia, and it's tearing her apart."

Amelia took a sip from the glass Erika had placed on Derek's desk and tried to tamp down the anger that had bubbled to the surface. As a librarian, she'd seen all too often the damaged Littles—and children—who escaped from the pain of their daily lives through reading. "What can I do?"

"I've spoken to her cousin on the phone—he referred her—and to be honest I think what she needs more than anything else is security. Someone who's not going to be changeable at a moment's notice; who's not going to turn up drunk and berate her verbally. Someone who won't mind reading her stories; it seems like she's never really had someone to read her stories."

That was a crime. All Littles deserved to be read to, if they wanted it.

"But, Amelia, she's not looking for a Mommy."

Amelia snorted. "I've told you many a time, Derek, I'm not looking for a Little of my own. I'm quite satisfied with my job and also lending a helping hand where necessary."

"Of course."

He didn't say anything further on the subject, but Amelia couldn't quite shift the feeling that Master Derek Hawkins was up to his old matchmaking ways.

"And one final thing, I'll give you her file to read, but she's on no corporal punishment, and if she is naughty, she should be referred to yourself, or me if you're not available."

That was a surprise. It was pretty standard practice at the Ranch for Littles to be subjected to punishments by any of the Bigs. This Mandi must have left a big impression on Derek Hawkins.

"No corporal punishments?"

"You'll see when you meet her, Amelia; she's so anxious that getting her to open up to even one or two of us is going to be a mission. I don't want her petrified of every Big she walks past. I want her to be able to trust people, and to be able to lean on you—if you're open to it."

"I'm open." She was curious, she had to admit. It had been a long time since she'd seen Derek look this concerned about a guest. "If she's that anxious, maybe we should encourage her to see one of the counselors?"

"It's one of the conditions of her stay," he explained, and she nodded.

She did like how he took his role so seriously, looking

after all the souls who came into his life. It sounded like Mandi had found exactly who she needed to find.

"You'll take me to see her?"

"Yes, she's up in the Guest Wing with Sadie. Sadie's taken quite the shine to her; more protective over her than I've seen her be over anyone in quite some time."

The entrance to the Guest Wing was just across the foyer from Derek's office, and Amelia had forgotten how luxurious the suites were.

"We upgraded her," said Derek quietly as they entered. "She doesn't know and I'd rather not tell her."

The room was light and airy and they followed the sound of laughter round the corner to where Amelia could see Sadie sitting on a couch watching *Fraggle Rock* on the television.

"Where's Mandi, angel?" asked Derek.

"She's over here, Daddy," replied Sadie brightly, and as Amelia walked round, she caught sight of dark red hair, spilling over one of the seat cushions of the couch.

"Hello," said a quiet voice.

Amelia paused, arrested by big gray eyes blinking up at her. "Well, hello there, Miss Mandi," she said, and slipped down to sit by the couch. "I hear you're interested in coming to work in my Littles' Library?"

An enthusiastic pair of nods came from both women on the couch. From the way Mandi was clutching a teddy bear so tightly in her arms, it appeared he was adding his agreement with his own nod. "I've worked in a bookshop before, and I'm really good at organizing stock. What kinds of books do you have in the library?" Mandi asked.

"Most of our books are children's books, from board books and picture books, all the way up to YA for the Middles among us."

More nodding.

"But we don't just have books; we also have lots of

boardgames, and a whole section for art supplies, and people can order them to be delivered to their rooms as well. We've got a library catalogue, which people can log into from their phones, and it's very peaceful."

"It sounds like heaven," breathed Mandi.

Amelia found herself transfixed by the way her soft plumpness moved when she exhaled in a long drawn out sigh. The woman was adorable; short and round and more than a little heavenly herself. Amelia wasn't one for instant attraction, but she couldn't help but think about how all that softness would feel in her arms.

"I do run a tight ship though; returns reshelved as quickly as possible, and I like to rotate the book displays."

Mandi nodded, all serious earnestness. "Of course! And do you often order in new stock? There are lots of amazing books that I'd love to recommend."

The Little Library had just had a delivery of new books the previous week; Amelia had ordered them in herself. They definitely didn't need more new books any time soon.

"I'm working on a new order now; what books would you recommend?"

"I've got some *amazing* picture books that I just know the Littles will love."

"How did you know that they're what I'm planning to order in?" Amelia steadfastly avoided meeting Derek's eye. He knew exactly how big the order of picture books she'd just received was, and she didn't need any of his knowing glances. Books clearly made Mandi happy, and suddenly she realized that there wasn't much she wouldn't do to make the other woman happy. If that included allowing the young woman to participate by recommending they order even more picture books, so be it. Amelia knew that while Derek had just paid for the most recent order of picture books, he wouldn't make so much as a fuss if ordering even more helped one of his guests feel happy and secure at Rawhide Ranch. It wouldn't stop him from noticing how taken she might or might not be with the other woman. "It sounds like you would be the perfect person to come and help me in the library. And you're staying for a week?"

Another nod, this one more vigorous than the last. She was just too cute!

"That's lovely. Now, Mandi, Master Derek told me you've agreed to two conditions while you're staying with us: that you'll have a counseling session with Dr. Denton; and that you'll allow one person to be in charge of your wellbeing. How would you feel about allowing me to take on that role?"

All of a sudden, Mandi slipped off the couch and onto the floor so she could meet Amelia's eyes straight on. She didn't say anything at first, gray eyes searching, searching, searching.

"I have some conditions of my own," she said, her voice quiet in the vastness of the suite.

"Go ahead."

"No shouting at me, please. It makes me jump and my autism makes me very sensitive to sound." She turned her head and lifted her hair from her neck to show where a cute rose-gold-colored earplug was nestled in her ear. "I often wear these in my day to day life; they're designed so I can hear people close to me, but they shut out background chat and noise."

"That seems very sensible. Good girl for looking after yourself like that. And that's fine by me; no shouting it is."

A pink flush rose up Mandi's neck until even the tip of her nose turned pink. So, she liked "good girl". Amelia made an internal note.

"I don't want to spend time around people who are drinking. It's okay if people drink, I'm not judging anyone, but I just—"

"I don't really drink," said Amelia. "It's forbidden in the Littles' Wing and that's where I spend a lot of my time. I've been known to have a glass of wine with dinner, but if that makes you uncomfortable I simply won't."

"Oh." Mandi's eyes widened in surprise. "Just like that?"

"Just like that."

Mandi ducked her head, and Amelia fought the urge to put her finger beneath that chin and make her princess hold her head up high.

"Okay, and then lastly, I don't think I want corporal punishments."

"Yes, Master Derek has expressed that to me already." That was fine with Amelia. She could think of far more creative ways to punish naughty Littles than spanking.

"It's not that"—and here Mandi lowered her voice, as if Sadie and Derek weren't right there and could hear every word—"I don't *like* impact play, I just don't want it to be associated with badness."

Amelia couldn't help her smile. Damn, Mandi was adorable. "I understand."

And then Mandi realized exactly what she'd said and started panicking. "I mean, I'm not saying that we would, or even that… I, oh goodness, I just—"

Amelia placed a finger on Mandi's lips and the redhead quieted. "I assume nothing. Thank you for sharing your boundaries with me, and that's totally okay. I don't need to resort to impact play to come up with totally wicked punishments." Amelia then smiled, to show she was half joking, and that there really was nothing to be scared of whatsoever.

But it was when Mandi smiled back at her, that Amelia knew she was totally lost.

CHAPTER 4

Miss Grayson wasn't what Mandi had expected. She'd been expecting someone stern and strict, not this blonde in a suit with cropped hair and a warm smile that made her toes want to wiggle.

And yes, she was talking about punishments, but somehow Mandi knew that they wouldn't make her feel degraded or all torn up inside. She understood that Miss Grayson would be stern and strict when she needed to be, but her words promised so many books.

"Can we visit the library now?" she asked, eager to get started.

Miss Grayson glanced at her watch, "Well, it's nearly lunchtime, so how about we grab some food first, and get to know each other a bit better."

Food was good. Mandi liked food. But… "I'm okay without lunch!"

The look that Miss Grayson shot her said otherwise.

"Ummm… I will have lunch?"

"You will definitely have lunch."

Master Derek chuckled behind them, and Mandi swiveled to look at him. "Oh, no," he said, "Miss Grayson's in charge now. No looking at me for respite. Come on, angel," he added to Sadie, "I think you need to have a nap before your lunch."

Sadie pulled a face. "Fine, but only because it'll mean I'll be refreshed later for our Little search." She threw herself off the couch to hug Mandi. "We're going to be the best of friends, Mandi, I promise. And if you ever feel scared or overwhelmed and Miss Grayson isn't around, you and Beau can always come find me."

"Thank you," Mandi said quietly. She'd been so isolated for so long that she'd almost forgotten what it was like to have a friend who looked out for you. And the fact Sadie had included Beau made her feel even more welcome. "Really."

Sadie met her eyes for a moment, her own clouded with sadness, and smiled a sad smile that implied that she knew exactly what Mandi had just been thinking, and then the sadness was gone and Sadie was up and off in a flurry of movement that made Master Derek and Miss Grayson laugh.

"Now," said Miss Grayson, when they were alone, "how about we move up onto the couch here and chat a bit. Would you like to do lunch in one of restaurants?"

Mandi shook her head vigorously. Restaurants had yummy food, but they also had lots of people. And people meant strangers. And strangers usually meant noise. Lots and lots of noise.

She didn't think she could cope with lots of noise right now.

"Okay, petal, but you're going to have to use your words and share what you're thinking with me."

Mandi sent Miss Grayson a beseeching, silent look to no avail.

"Nope. Sorry to disappoint you, but puppy dog eyes don't work on me. I'm too used to naughty Littles trying to coopt my art supplies for pranks. Come now, what's going on in that pretty little head of yours?"

"Too noisy," Mandi said. Luckily the short sentence seemed to suffice.

"I guess that is the case, but luckily all the eateries here deliver room service. What do you fancy, and no," the other woman said pointedly, "I will not choose for you. This is your first meal here and by the sounds of it you've had a fairly stressful morning. There's Mexican, Italian, American, and the café does sandwiches and treats. Take your pick."

Picking for herself from a takeout menu was something Mandi was well acquainted with. "Maybe a chicken salad sandwich? And a treat for dessert?"

"Absolutely," but when Miss Grayson turned to the phone to dial room service, Mandi caught the back of her shirt. "Yes?"

"Takeout is nice, but I like to cook too, and I think this suite has a kitchenette." She peered over the top of the couch, and round the room until she spotted it just past the dining area. Smiling she pointed and added, "So maybe we order room service today, but I can get some food in to cook too?"

"I'm sure that's possible. If you come up with a list, I'll make sure that Chef Connor gets it and can fill a box with your choice of ingredients."

"Do you think Sadie would like it if I cooked her mac and cheese?"

"Well, I know that Sadie loves Chef Connor's mac and cheese, so…"

Mandi didn't even hear the end of the sentence. She could feel herself drawing back from the idea, knowing it was unlikely she could ever live up to a fancy chef's mac and cheese.

"Mandi," Miss Grayson crouched down to meet her

eyes. "I think Sadie would *love* it, and I believe it's a lovely idea to include your new friend."

The panic inside her subsided, and Mandi wiggled in her seat. The more time she spent around Miss Grayson the more she felt her Little peeking out curiously. She swung her feet experimentally, to see if that would coax her Little out, but instead her Little retreated, and she sighed.

"Is everything okay?"

This time, Mandi's voice was louder than it had been all day, and far more frustrated. "I'm just… the whole *point* of coming here was to find my Little and she just won't come out. I've lost her. I've fucking lost her and it's my own fucking fault."

Silence followed her outburst, though Mandi would swear the naughty words were reverberating louder and louder around the room. Mandi wanted to dive under a blanket and hide. Her very first day and she'd already broken one of the core rules of Rawhide Ranch. Her eyes stung with tears that threatened to fall, and she pulled herself up and into the corner of the couch, making herself as small as she possibly could.

"I'm sorry," she whispered, but her voice trembled, and she didn't dare look at Miss Grayson. "I know I'm not supposed to swear, but—"

"No, you're not," Miss Grayson agreed without hesitation as she sat back down on the couch next to her. Her voice didn't sound angry, and it wasn't raised.

Mandi snuck a flicker of a look up at the other woman's face, and she looked sad. Well, that sucked. As well as cussing, she'd now made Miss Grayson sad. The tears brimmed in Mandi's eyes and she blinked them away in frustration.

"I think we possibly need a time out from all the talks about your Little. How about, while we wait for room service, you unpack the suitcase that Moses has brought up, and put all your clothes away tidily in the closet."

Slightly stunned and confused, Mandi said, "You're not going to punish me?"

"Oh I am," said Miss Grayson, "Just not how you'd expect. For every three items of clothing you put away, I want you to tell me one thing you like about yourself. You swore because you were angry at yourself, so I want you to soften that emotion and show yourself some love."

That made Mandi turn and look at her face on. "Wait, what? It's okay, I was only… I mean, I don't want to—"

"Are you safewording?"

Mandi stared at her. Was she? She couldn't remember the last time someone had spoken to her so directly about the way she spoke about herself. It was nice, but unsettling.

"Mandi, are you familiar with the traffic-light system used to help you feel secure and safe?"

Mandi nodded. She'd used it previously with her ex—sometimes with good results. Remembering she was expected to use her words, she pictured the three color choices in her head: red for stop right now; yellow for pause and check in; green for all good. She took a moment and considered each of them before saying, "Green, Miss. I'm green, I think."

"You think?"

"No, I know. I'm green."

"Good girl. Come on, I'll come with you and you can tell me all of the lovely things I can look forward to seeing for myself."

CHAPTER 5

AMELIA DIDN'T KNOW how anyone could be cruel to little Mandi, even when she wasn't Little. The redhead was the most adorable thing the librarian had ever seen, perfectly folding and putting away her clothes and stumbling through an awkward list of things she liked about herself.

She'd started off hesitant, as if she couldn't think of anything at all, but eventually came up with quite the list—even if Amelia had to prompt her a few times.

Apparently Mandi was very good at organizing books, a good listener, kind, a great cook, and she liked her hair.

Amelia liked her hair too. There were almost golden strands among the red that glinted when the light caught them, and it looked as if she were sparkling.

When room service delivered their lunch, they sat at the table and ate together in relative quiet. It was actually rather lovely. She was so used to having to hush all the exuberant Littles who came bounding into her library, that it was refreshing not to have her ear talked off. Although if Mandi was doing the talking, she didn't think she'd mind.

Once they'd cleared the table and popped the dishes on

the tray in the corridor outside the door to the suite, they set off toward the Littles' Wing and the Littles' Library.

As they turned into the foyer, the noise level rose, and Amelia paused. "Are your earplugs in, petal?"

Mandi checked her ears and nodded and smiled.

"Excellent. Well, it's lunch time so a lot of the Littles will be coming out of classes and it might be a bit noisy."

Mandi's eyes got wide and slightly panicky, and Amelia found herself offering her hand to the other woman.

"You can hold my hand if that would help?"

Mandi stared at Amelia's hand for a long time, before cautiously accepting the offer, fingers entwining and interlinking. Mandi's skin was cool against her palm, and Amelia squeezed once to reassure the Little before they headed across the foyer.

There was a full giggle of Littles running around, causing havoc. Callie, Britt and Megan were heading toward the café, talking quietly, and Sadie was holding court over by the fireplace. She waved at them, and Amelia could sense Mandi trying to work out how to wave back without dropping Beau. When Mandi finally settled on letting Beau do the waving by simply wagging him up and down, Amelia had to smile. It was just too adorable for words.

But when they turned into the Littles' Wing, Nanny J and Miss Price were walking down the corridor together and both wore expressions that reminded Amelia of how thunder must appear before it let loose and roiled loudly across the sky. Amelia wasn't entirely certain which Littles had decided to prank two of the strictest Ranch employees, but she instantly felt empathy for the culprits' bottoms.

Mandi, on the other hand, froze and shrank back, her Beau carrying-hand creeping up until she was hugging Amelia's arm. The librarian could feel Mandi trembling.

"Who's this then?" asked Nanny J, and Amelia felt a

twinge of annoyance at quite how stern the Head of the Littles' Wing sounded.

"This is Mandi Travers, who's coming to work with me in the Littles' Library." She didn't intend to step forward so that Mandi could slip behind her, but somehow it just happened.

Nanny J's face softened at Mandi's name, and she tilted her head to look around Amelia's shoulder. "Hey, Mandi, I'm sorry if we scared you. I'm Nanny J, and this is Miss Price who teaches the preschoolers."

"Hi there, Mandi," said Miss Price, equally as gently.

"He-hello," proffered Mandi, anxiously.

Amelia felt pride welling up inside of her. Her little girl was trying so hard.

Nanny J continued, "There was a prank, so we're off to find the troublemakers responsible. Master Derek said that Mandi's your charge during her stay?"

"Yes, that's right." Amelia squeezed Mandi's hand again, and she felt the body pressed up against her relax slightly.

"Great, we'll send her to the library if she gets lost. And, Mandi," she added, Mandi's body stiffening in response. "Welcome to Rawhide Ranch. You're in good hands with Miss Grayson, and everyone knows that she's looking after you, so you don't need to be scared of any of us. No one here's going to get angry with you—maybe just disappointed if you're naughty."

"I'm a good girl," said Mandi tentatively, her voice almost lisping slightly.

Amelia froze, not wanting to scare off this display of Littleness.

"Mommy Grayson says so."

Mommy Grayson.

Nanny J and Miss Price hid their surprise better than Amelia did, who looked down at the short woman next to her. "Mandi—"

"I'm sorry!" she interrupted, the cute lisp disappearing. "I should have asked, we didn't talk, I mean I—"

Amelia's index finger kissed Mandi's lips and the torrent of words paused. "No panicking, petal, I was just surprised. Master Derek said you weren't looking for a Mommy."

Mandi dropped her head and fiddled with her top. This time Amelia did place her finger under Mandi's chin and lift it until they made eye contact. "Chin up, princess."

"I'm afraid it just came out," said Mandi, apologetically.

"Nanny J, Miss Price, we're going to head into the library," said Amelia, determined to sit down and have this conversation someplace they wouldn't have other people listening. "Come on, petal, let's have this talk properly."

CHAPTER 6

Mandi had messed up. She knew it. You didn't call people by honorifics without speaking to them about it first. But she'd felt so small and…

She'd felt small.

She'd felt *Little*.

All of a sudden, she wanted to jump up and down and sing. She'd found her Little! Her Little wasn't lost, not completely, just hibernating. And then she looked up at the woman who made her feel safe being Little, and sighed. What if she'd messed up completely, and Miss Grayson didn't want to look after her after all. What if she never got to be Little again?

The hand holding hers squeezed again. "Stop panicking. I can hear your brain snakes."

"My brain snakes?"

"Yes, the squirrelly bits of your brain that say horrible things to you, and make you doubt yourself and your actions. Brain snakes slithering around. Two-forked tongues flickering about and hissing vile things into our hearts." She gave an exaggerated shudder that echoed exactly how Mandi felt at such an image before adding,

"Even us Bigs get them." She looked down at Mandi and smiled. "I'm not angry and I'm not cross; I just want us to have a grown-up conversation about what we want this to be, so we're both on the same page."

Then she squeezed Mandi's hand again, before the brain snakes could resume their hissing. "And just to be clear, for any residual brain snakes, I liked it. When you called me Mommy."

Mandi had liked it too. It had felt *right*. It had never quite felt that right before, and she realized she wanted to cling on to that with both hands.

But all that was shoved aside when she walked into the Littles' Library and saw all of the books.

Shelves and shelves and shelves full of lovely books. Her eyes sparkled and then she was off running to look at this display here and that pile of boardgames over there. The library was big and safe and she couldn't help the happy wiggles that escaped. She ran up and down the stacks, and it wasn't until she paused, panting in the center of the room, that she noticed Miss Grayson leaning against the checkout counter and smiling at her.

"I know," Mandi said, contritely. "Grown-up conversation to be had. But I couldn't help it. Look at the books!"

The librarian huffed a laugh and then beckoned her over to what Mandi assumed was the librarian's office.

"Now normally," said Miss Grayson, "I wouldn't recommend having this kind of conversation in your workplace, but Rawhide is slightly different, and I know you're here on a trial run. And none of the Littles dare come in here when the door's shut, so we'll have plenty of privacy."

She led Mandi over to a dinky couch in the corner of the small office, and they sat down. "So, petal, what's going on with you?"

This time, for some reason, Mandi didn't have any

problems with her words. They weren't stuttered out, and they weren't waterfalling out. "I think I went a bit Little."

"Mmhmm. And what do you think brought that on?"

She thought back to that moment in the corridor, and saw stern, cross faces. "I think I got a bit scared of Nanny J and Miss Price."

"Oh, pickle, scared?"

"They looked really cross!"

Miss Grayson took Mandi's hands in hers, and she felt the tension in her shoulders lessen, just a smidgeon. "Pranks are pretty commonplace in the Littles' Wing, and the Littles do them, knowing that the consequences are likely to be a red bottom once they're caught. They know and though they don't enjoy spanks in the moment, I have it on good authority that they don't mind them. They wouldn't be here if they did, or at least, it would be written into their agreement no spanks for them."

Mandi nodded slowly. "I don't think it's the idea of spanks that I mind, it's the idea of someone spanking because they're cross."

"Oh that's different. Very rarely do Bigs here spank when they're actually cross. If someone is really cross, we'd take a time out or some space, and calm down first. Usually, we'd only be really cross if the Littles were putting themselves or others in danger. The rest of the time we're just amused by their attempts at being sassy."

Mandi took a few minutes to process that, and she did admit that it made her feel much better to know that punishments weren't delivered in anger.

"I understand. But I don't think I realized that when I saw them, and they made me feel scared. They were really nice when they spoke to me though, and that made me feel bad about being scared."

"Oh, sweetheart," Miss Grayson brushed a curl from her face. "It's okay to feel scared sometimes. And if we know why, then we can decide about what to do with that information. Do you think that's why you called me Mommy? Because you were scared?"

Mandi nodded vigorously. "Yes, and you feel super safe, and I knew that if people were being really scary, you'd look after me."

"I would, petal, I really would."

"Ummm… Miss Grayson, how would you feel if I called you Mommy Grayson again? And maybe for my time here?"

The librarian paused, and Mandi braced herself for rejection. She could deal with it; it'd hurt, but she'd been through worse. It was just a small no, and small words didn't have to hurt and…

"I think I'd prefer it if you called me Mommy Amelia or just Mommy."

Oh. She hadn't been expecting that.

"Amelia? Is that your name?"

The blonde woman nodded. "Yes. Mommy Grayson sounds nice, but it's also really formal, and everyone calls me Miss Grayson. Some of the Tops, and Master Derek, call me Amelia sometimes, but it's usually Miss and my surname. If you're going to call me Mommy, I'd like you to use my first name."

"Mommy Amelia," Mandi tried it out. The words felt nice on her tongue, soft "Ms" bursting from pressed lips. "I like it. How… I mean… what… I mean…"

Mommy Amelia laughed. "Are you trying to ask what I'd like this dynamic to look like?"

Mandi smiled her agreement.

"Well, it's up to you really. Some Littles want to be babies, some want to be Little all the time, some want to slip in and out. Some want non-sexual kink and others want sexual-kink. It all depends on the person."

"What would you like?" Mandi asked, curious.

"Oh no," laughed Mommy Amelia, "You're too much of a people pleaser for me to answer that question. You're the Little; you set the boundaries."

Setting her own boundaries; wasn't that a novice concept.

"Can I think about it for a little while? This morning I thought I'd lost my Little forever, and now we're discussing a dynamic. I think I need to process it a bit first."

"Of course, petal," said Mommy Amelia, "you take as long as you need."

CHAPTER 7

When Mandi needed to think, really think, she organized. So when she needed to process something of this magnitude, she asked Mommy Amelia if she could shelve the returned books.

A children's library—or at least the fiction section—wasn't so much organized by the Dewey Decimal System, but rather by age and then alphabetically or by topic. Mandi headed straight for the YA fiction section. Picture books were perfect for organizing displays, but when she wanted to go into automatic mode and let her brain do its thing, she alphabetized.

As her fingers ran along book spines, finding the right home for each story, she thought.

She'd thought her Little was lost, and while it wasn't entirely lost, Mandi knew her Little wasn't entirely comfortable being back, either. And also, she was scared of being Little all the time; it would be too harsh a transition when she had to leave.

Her stomach clenched and her mouth dried. The idea of leaving… but that was a week away, and she had plenty of time before then.

Moving quickly through the stacks, the YA books were all shelved in no time. She went on to Middle Grade next.

And she loved working with books, but she didn't always want to be Little when she did that; she already had ideas for a books and boardgames display, and maybe even a workshop they could run. Being fully Little in a work environment meant she wouldn't be able to have control over the one thing she'd also managed to keep for herself—her love of books.

Okay, so slipping between Big and Little seemed like what she really wanted.

And what about other Big activities, like kink and sex?

Surreptitiously, she peeped around the corner of one of the bookshelves to gaze at Mommy Amelia.

The tall woman wore a neat suit, that didn't seem too starchy or overly pressed. There was a flow to the lines of it that flattered her figure, and the idea of holding on to the lapels of that blazer as Mommy Amelia made her come...

Flushed, Mandi spun back around and leaned against the shelves, breathing deeply. So she might be interested in sex with Mommy Amelia. A teensy bit.

A lot.

Blushing even hotter at the inner truth she was attempting to ignore, she finished shelving the books on her cart, and then pushed it over to where Mommy Amelia sat behind the check-in desk.

"I think I know what I want, Mommy," she said.

"Oh yes?"

There was a flash of something in Mommy Amelia's eyes that made Mandi go all giggly.

Mommy just waited patiently until all of Mandi's giggles had died down, and then asked, "You okay there, petal?"

She nodded, smiling happily. "Yes. I have books and a

Mommy and-and..." Mandi took a deep breath and then started wiggling, "And I have the happy wiggles!"

"Not the happy wiggles!" Mommy Amelia came over and wiggled with her a bit, which made Mandi giggle even more.

When she was all wiggled out, she walked into her Mommy's office and then looked behind her expectantly.

"Oh I'm *so* sorry, petal dear, I can see I've been summoned!"

That made her want to start giggling again, but she put on her serious face instead and sat down, haughtily gesturing toward the chair behind the desk. "You may sit."

Mommy Amelia looked as though she wanted to laugh herself, but she sat down and waited to hear what Mandi had to say. It was more than Mandi had dared hope for and absolutely delicious.

"I think that I'm not ready to be Little all of the time, and I'm not sure I'll ever be ready. I won't always feel comfortable being Little in front of people I don't know, and I also like the feeling of being Big, particularly when I'm working."

"That makes sense," said Mommy Amelia. "You're clearly very good at working in a book environment, and it makes you happy to do so. If it's not broke, why fix it?"

"But I do want to try being Little more, and to encourage my Little to maybe come out in my day-to-day life. I'm curious to see when she's going to want to come out."

"Me too," said Mommy Amelia, and her smile almost took Mandi's breath away.

"And that's the other thing," Mandi said, trying to keep the confident tone, and banishing the encroaching brain snakes into the darkest recesses of her mind. "Kink is a Big thing for me, and I like it, or at least, I think I do? I don't know if you'd be… open to maybe exploring some of that with me?"

Mommy Amelia stayed very still at that question, and Mandi got the impression that she was trying very hard to appear laidback. "I think—ahem—yes, I would be open to that. What kind of kink would you be interested in?"

"Sexual." Mandi had never owned her own desire in such a forthright, open way before. She'd always tiptoed around what she wanted, content to just follow what others desired of her. But now, faced with this beautiful woman, she knew what she wanted. "I would very much like to explore… that, with you. If you're open to—"

"Yes." The word almost burst forth from Mommy Amelia, and it made them both laugh. "Yes, sweet girl, I would most definitely be open to that."

"I don't think I want to play publicly; the Dungeon sounds fun and all, but also a bit scary."

"I don't think it would necessarily suit your sensory needs, petal. But if there's something you particularly would like to try, we can always use one of the private playrooms. Or even see if we can have an apparatus delivered to my house or your suite for a scene."

Mandi felt her eyes widen. "They can do that?"

Amelia smiled and nodded. "You'll find there isn't much that can't be made to happen here. Rawhide Ranch is very good at fulfilling all sorts of fantasies Bigs and Littles can dream up."

"Wow," Mandi said softly, images popping in and out of her head as she nodded. "That all sounds… um, really good." Her face grew warm again and she wondered just how pink her cheeks must be by now. "Um, can… um, I mean may I…"

"What is it?" Mommy Amelia asked when Mandi couldn't seem to finish her question.

"Could I… may I have a kiss please?" Mandi asked so

softly she wasn't sure she'd spoken the request out loud, until she saw her Mommy's smile.

"Oh, darling, of course you can."

They rose at the same time, and Mandi dropped her eyes, laughing awkwardly. But then Mommy Amelia was striding forward, and standing close to her, so close that Mandi could count the buttons on her blouse.

"You come up to my chin, sweet girl; perfectly sized for me."

Mandi looked up into dark brown eyes, searching for something intangible, and when Mommy Amelia's lips curled up in a smile that brightened her eyes into a delicious caramel color, Mandi saw it, raised onto her tiptoes and kissed the librarian.

CHAPTER 8

Mandi was everything Amelia could have dreamed of.

Soft, cupid bow lips pressed against hers with a gentle eagerness that almost undid her, and then Amelia was sliding her fingers through the thick strands of the redhead's hair, cradling her head between her hands as Amelia kissed her back.

And then Mandi sighed. She *sighed*, like she was some heroine in a romance novel, and just melted against Amelia; hips and tits molding themselves against her. In that moment she wanted nothing more than every inch of clothing covering Mandi banished, so that she could slide her hands down to hold that bare ass and pull her girl tight in against her.

"Ahem."

Amelia released Mandi's lips and turned to find Sadie at the door to her office, which she'd left open for some unknown reason.

Grinning cheekily, Sadie said, "Miss Grayson, Daddy wanted to know whether Mandi had settled in okay. What should I tell him?"

Mandi blushed bright red, and backed away, almost tripping over a pile of books in her hurry.

Amelia caught her before she could fall and pulled her in close. Full romance novel vibes of her own went into action right then and there. Meeting Mandi's eyes, she smiled and said, "Hey, petal, it's all good. It's only Sadie, being mischievous as ever." Turning her head toward the door once more, she added, "And don't you know you should knock, Sadie Hawkins?"

Sadie's grin spread even wider. "I did. You were just too… um, occupied to hear it."

"Oh." Well, it wasn't Sadie's fault; she'd been kissing her sweet girl into oblivion. "Mandi, would you like to go with Sadie and tell her and Master Derek all about what we've discussed?"

Mandi's eyes were wide even before she began to shake her head from side to side. "Do I have to? Can't you do it?"

Amelia had to hold firm, or she'd find herself giving in to every demand that came from those sweet, sweet lips.

"No, little one, not this time. It's important for you to do it, because it's a change to the form you filled out." She waited for a couple of breaths before clarifying, "If what we discussed is truly what you'd like to explore going forward that is."

"It is," Mandi said without a moment's hesitation.

"It is?" Sadie's eyes were wide.

Mandi nodded, her delight painted across her face.

Amelia smiled and dropped a kiss on top of her girl's head. "Okay then, you hop along and do that, and then maybe head out to play with Sadie afterward for a bit. We can talk about what you're going to be doing in the library when you're working after you get back."

"Okay, Mommy."

Amelia was delighted with the immediate address, as well as noticing Mandi was the one to link arms with Sadie this time, and as the two of them headed off together, Mandi was actually contributing to the conversation. She was so proud of her girl.

Her girl.

Hadn't it only been that morning that she'd told Derek she wasn't looking for a Little of her own?

Instead, this parcel of anxious adorableness had landed in her lap—almost literally—and now she was second guessing every decision she'd ever made.

It wasn't like Amelia hadn't played with people before. She'd even toyed with the idea of having a Little of her own. But her life had been hard, and her family less than supportive when she'd come out, and she just didn't know what being a good Caregiver was.

Well, perhaps she hadn't originally, not with her own horrendous examples of parents at least. But she'd seen Derek look after so many of the Littles and submissives who'd walked through those iron gates, seen him fall in love and look after Sadie in an entirely different way.

She knew now what it took to keep someone you loved safe, and maybe it was those observations and knowledge that now changed the way she was seeing Mandi.

Before, she'd have argued she didn't have the time or the inclination to take one Little under her wing, but Derek asked for very few things, and he'd given her so much. Given her the librarian job, an apartment, and then a house when she'd decided to stay on at Rawhide permanently. She was paid well, fed well, and wanted for very little.

Apart from a Little.

She hadn't Dommed anyone, one on one, in a long time, and hadn't slept with anyone for even longer. It just hadn't held much of an interest for her. Her demisexuality meant that she rarely felt sexual attraction to strangers. She could appreciate beauty—sure—but that didn't mean she wanted to sleep with someone just for the hell of it.

She needed to form a bond, a connection with someone before she'd begin to feel any kind of sexual attraction.

And somehow, that connection was there with Mandi.

Ten years working at Rawhide and zilch.

One morning with Mandi and her entire life had been turned upside down.

Mandi, who was sweet and kind, and loved books and wanted to cook a meal for her new friend, and who was leaving in a week.

Fuck.

The reality of that sunk in and Amelia thought she might be sick. One week? One week was all she got to spend with this woman, this woman with red hair and gray eyes that spoke of a soul a thousand years old?

A week couldn't possibly be enough.

But it would have to be.

She would fill this week with a thousand memories; would make it the perfect week for her perfect girl; and then send her off into the world, whole and loved. Even if she knew her own heart would be broken.

CHAPTER 9

Sadie was almost bouncing with excitement as they walked down the corridor toward Master Derek's office. She seemed almost more excited than Mandi did at the prospect of Mandi having found a Mommy in Amelia Grayson.

"This is amazing, Mandi. And your Little! You found her!"

"Kind of," said Mandi. "I mean, she's definitely around, but I don't think she's all the way back just yet." But she was skipping, and she did feel happy, and Beau was still in her hand, but not clutched quite as tightly as when she'd arrived that morning.

Sadie opened the door to Master Derek's office without knocking, to Mandi's wide-eyed astonishment, and the admonishment that he gave his angel made Mandi giggle instead of cower.

"Oh yes," he said, turning to look at her. "I see our Little Lady is a little more giggly than she was this morning. I take it that you're settling in with Miss Grayson okay?"

Mandi almost bounced on the spot, and some happy wiggles escaped. "Yes, Mommy Amelia is *amazing*."

"Mommy Ame—well," he said, recovering rather quickly, "I see things have changed quite a bit since this morning. I thought you weren't looking for a Mommy or a Daddy, Mandi?"

"I wasn't," she said, moving to sit in one of the large leather chairs. "May I sit?"

"You may," Master Derek said. Sadie went to sit down on the other, but he raised a hand. "Not you, angel. You may turn and face the bookshelf over there and consider why we knock on doors instead of bursting through them."

Sadie pulled a face at him, and then hurriedly ran to the bookshelf when he went to get up out of his chair.

"And no turning round, or I'll spank you and then make you stand in the corner all over again."

He winked at Mandi, and she hid a giggle. It was like Mommy Amelia had said, Sadie didn't mind her punishments, even if she gave exaggerated sighs or rolled her eyes about it.

"So, why don't you explain what changed your mind."

"To be honest," she said, "it was my Little. I got a bit nervous around some of the other Bigs, and my Little came out, and she clung to Miss Grayson and called her Mommy."

Master Derek looked thoughtful. "And what did Miss Grayson say about that?"

Blushing, Mandi smiled. "She said she liked it, but we also sat down and had a grown-up talk about it too, so my Little wasn't making all my decisions for me. And then I even took some extra time to work out what it is that I want from our dynamic."

"And what is that?"

"I don't want to be Little all of the time. Even if I was in a place like this where I technically could be if I wanted, she's still really hurt and scared, and doesn't want to come out around lots of people. And I also like being Big, particularly when I'm at work. And also when... well, um..." she ducked her head to hide the color she felt flooding into her cheeks but not before seeing Master Derek smile.

"Ah yes, *those* times. You're happy about these changes you've decided to make?"

"Absolutely. I don't think I've ever been surer of anything!" She lifted her head and nodded as to make sure he was clear about how sure she was.

He looked at her then, the kindly expression on his face very gentle. "I do want to say though, you're only booked in to stay for a week. It might be quite difficult for you—and for your Little—to find a Mommy and then have to say goodbye to her."

Mandi must have blanched, because he poured her a glass of water, and spoke quietly while she drank it. "I'm not saying don't explore this connection with Miss Grayson—in fact, I think it will be very good for the both of you—I'm just saying be careful of your heart, and of your Little."

"I will. Thank you though; you've been very kind. Both of you," she added, turning to include Sadie in that statement. "I was wondering actually, if the two of you are not too busy tomorrow night, would you like to have dinner in my suite? I make a mean mac and cheese."

Sadie started bouncing up and down on the spot, though wisely remained silent and continued to steadfastly face the bookshelves.

"That would be lovely, thank you, Mandi."

She beamed.

"But you do know you don't have to earn our friendship. You have it, whether you invite us around for dinner or not. And we are more looking forward to the opportunity to spend more time with you, than we are the mac and cheese."

There was a muffled squeak from the corner.

Master Derek grinned. "Although," he admitted, "the mac and cheese is most certainly an added bonus."

CHAPTER 10

Sadie seemed fairly chipper when they left Master Derek's office, despite her stint by the bookshelf. "I'm sorry you got in trouble," Mandi offered.

"Oh that's okay," Sadie said. "He's just a bit of a grumpyguts sometimes. But I love him. Come on, let's go outside!"

She grabbed Mandi by the hand and dragged her laughing out into the sunshine. It was early afternoon and most of the other Littles were in class, so they had the whole playground to themselves.

Mandi headed straight for the swings. She might be afraid of heights, but for some reason that didn't apply to being on the swings. She could just soar up into the air, and then back down to safety.

The two of them challenged each other to go as high as they possibly could, leaning back and kicking their legs out. They weren't quiet though, and by the time a tall man in a black Stetson and shiny alligator-skin boots came to see what was going on, Mandi was in full Little mode.

"Miss Sadie, shouldn't you be in class?"

"Nope, it's okay, Chief, Daddy said I could take Mandi

out to play. She's new today. She's Miss Grayson's Little! Say hi, Mandi!"

"Hi, Mandi," Mandi echoed and giggled.

The Chief took his hat off and laughed. "You too are having quite a lot of fun but do remember that other people are in class. We shouldn't distract them."

"Sucks to be them!" said Sadie, and though Mandi didn't quite have the nerve to echo Sadie's sentiment, she did pipe up with a defiant "Yup!"

The Chief raised his eyebrows. "I think the two of you need to calm down and come off the swings now."

"Don't wanna," said Sadie, but she started to slow down her swing anyway.

Mandi, on the other hand, was having far too much fun to stop now. It had been so long since she'd been on swings, so long since she'd felt *free* that she simply leaned back and pumped her legs harder to drive the swing up higher.

The Chief took a step toward her swing, his face serious, and she flinched violently, releasing the chains and propelling herself backward off the swing. She heard Sadie's scream, and screwed her eyes tightly shut, waiting for the ground to come up and hit her in the face. Instead, she felt someone catch her, and set her down gently on the grass.

"Sadie, go and get Miss Grayson. Now."

Mandi heard Sadie speed off without a sound, and she slowly opened her eyes, blinking wildly. The Chief was leaning over her, with a look of relief on his face.

"Hey there, you gave me quite the shock. Maybe keep your bratting to when you're feet are solidly on the ground, yes?"

She nodded, and went to get up, but her legs were all trembly, and she stumbled backward.

"I got you," he said. "Hey, Amelia, Little Mandi's had a bit of a shock."

When Mandi saw the librarian striding across the playground toward her, she burst into tears. "Mommy!" she wailed.

In two quick steps, Mommy Amelia was by her side, putting her arms around Mandi and holding her close. "There, there, petal. You've had a shock, is all. You're okay." Then turning toward Chief Lawson, she asked, "What happened?"

Mandi hid her face in her Mommy's shoulder, too embarrassed to look at her while the Chief explained what had happened.

"Well, Sadie and Mandi were having a grand old time on the swings, but when I asked them to keep the noise down, they got a bit cheeky with me."

Mommy Amelia drew back and gave Mandi a look—no, not a look—she gave her the *Look*.

"And then when I told them to come off the swings, Sadie said she didn't want to, but did start slowing down, but Mandi here decided to go higher instead."

The Look intensified.

"And I think I must have startled her when I stepped forward to catch the swing, because she went tumbling back off it. I managed to catch her, and she didn't hit her head."

"It's not her fault," said Sadie. "She's so good, but her Little came out and she was happy, and I encouraged her to be cheeky!"

"You may well have done so," said Mommy Amelia, "but that doesn't mean Mandi doesn't know the difference between right and wrong."

Mandi's bottom lip was trembling and she was trying so so hard not to cry again, but if Mommy's disappointment was aimed in her direction *one more time*…

"I think," said Mommy Amelia, "that someone has had quite enough excitement for one day and should have a quiet evening in their room."

"On my own?" Mandi's plaintive wail broke out of her as well as another flood of tears at the thought of being abandoned. She knew she'd messed up, but the idea of being punished by being left totally alone upset her more than she could have possibly expected.

Mommy Amelia placed a kiss on her forehead. "No, petal, not on your own. I'm going to come and spend it with you. But it won't be all fun; there are consequences for one's actions."

Mandi knew that perhaps she should feel dread about the prospect of a punishment, but in reality, all she felt was relief. She wasn't going to have to decide what she was doing next, Mommy would decide. And when she was done with her punishment, she got to start afresh.

This sounded like exactly what she needed.

CHAPTER 11

They were both quiet, all the way back to Mandi's room.

All Amelia could do was replay in her head, over and over, the moment when Sadie had come bursting into the library, saying Mandi had fallen backward off the swings. She'd almost thrown up, and she'd certainly abandoned any attempt at decorum as she'd set off running down the corridor to the doors opening on to the playground.

The relief when she'd realized her little girl was okay, and then the calm determination to make sure her Little got some quiet time was all that had kept her from having a full-blown panic attack.

When they reached the door of Mandi's suite, Amelia opened the door silently, and waited for the other woman to walk through. She'd never seen such meekness, and it worried her.

"Mandi?"

"Yes, Mommy?"

"What's going on in that head of yours?"

Mandi fidgeted and didn't look up.

"Chin up, princess. Come on, what're you thinking?"

When her girl met her eyes, they were brimming with tears. "I made you angry!"

"Oh, sweetheart," she pulled Mandi into her arms, and held her there, feeling the Little's shoulders shake with sobs. She stroked her hair gently. "I'm not angry. You were naughty, and there are consequences for that, but I was more worried about you than angry."

"Yeah?"

"Yeah." She drew Mandi over to the couch and they both sat down. "You've had a big day today—coming to a place you didn't know; meeting new people; finding a Mommy—and you're clearly overtired."

The sad upturned face nodded.

"So, what we're going to do, is that I'm going to give you your punishment, and we're going to do that nice and quietly. And then afterward, we're going to order up some food for dinner, curl up and watch some television together, and then you're going to get an early night."

"Will you stay the night?"

As if she could refuse that request. "Yes, of course I will."

"Okay." The face turned stoic. "Hit me with the punishment. I can take it."

Silently, Amelia went to the kitchenette and got one large bowl and six smaller bowls, and then reached into the cupboard and found the small jar of sprinkles that could always be found among the hot-cocoa making supplies in a Rawhide Ranch kitchenette. Everyone knew that a mug of hot chocolate could help soothe or serve as a treat for Littles and Bigs alike. Carefully, she upturned the jar into the large bowl, and brought it into the living area.

She placed it on the table and Mandi looked at it curiously, but still Amelia didn't say anything.

Next she gathered up some cushions and pillows,

placed them on the floor in front of the couch, and gestured to Mandi.

Mandi slid off the couch, onto the cushions and waited patiently.

Gods her little girl was such a good little thing.

"Okay, I want you to separate the sprinkles out into their different colors, so you have one bowl for each color: red, orange, yellow, green, blue, pink. I'm being nice with white; you can keep those in the big bowl."

Mandi's eyes got wide. "I have to sort *all of them*, Mommy?"

"All of them," confirmed Amelia. "And while you're doing it, I want you to think really hard about things you can do to help regulate yourself when you're feeling overly tired, rather than just acting out."

Mandi nodded slowly, and then diligently turned and set about sorting the sprinkles.

It took her a good while; perhaps half an hour, and the two of them sat in companionable silence, Mandi at Amelia's feet.

Amelia had to stop herself quite a few times from offering to help, or from distracting her girl by patting her back or stroking her fingers through the red strands of hair. The consequence was clearly working because she could see the tension in Mandi's shoulders dissipate, and by the time her Little was done, Mandi was clearly much happier.

Amelia rose only to then sit on the floor next to her Little to scrutinize the bowls. Mandi had done it perfectly! Not a single sprinkle was in the wrong bowl.

"Beautifully done," she praised, and kissed Mandi on the cheek, delighting when the other woman blushed. And then, she poured each individual bowl back into the one large bowl and then funneled all the colorful sprinkles back into the original jar.

"But, Mommy!" protested Mandi, her wide-eyed gaze showing her disbelief that all her hard work was so easily undone.

"Now, now, little girl," she said. "Punishments are punishments."

Mandi screwed up her face adorably, and Amelia bopped her on the nose. "Yes, Mommy," she grumbled, but it was so cute that Amelia let it go.

"And now for the second part of your punishment, little girl, you need to tell me about all the things you can do when you're feeling overtired, instead of acting out."

Mandi's screwed up face was a thinking face this time. "I can run my wrists under cold water! That usually helps. Also, I can get blankets and stuffies and curl up and be a cozy bug in a rug."

"Both excellent options," agreed Amelia, mentally taking notes for the next time Mandi got overly tired, so that she could help prompt her.

"Maybe a nap, but I don't really like naps."

Amelia looked unconvinced at that answer. "Naps are good for tired Little princesses."

"I *know*, but that doesn't mean that I like them. There are always too many books to read and sleeping feels like a waste of reading time."

"Well, you'll be getting plenty of sleeps while you're here. We can't have you getting overly tired and endangering yourself."

"This is true." Mandi's voice had slipped into her Little cadence now. "But, Mommy, all of those are good things to do when I'm at home or in my room; they're harder when I'm out and about."

"This is very true," said Amelia. "Can you think of anything that would help when you're out and about? You've explained that you're autistic, so do you—is it called stimming? Do you stim?"

"Ooooo…" Mandi wriggled on her cushion. "Yes! I stim automatically so often that I always forget about it as a self-regulating tool. Aren't you clever, Mommy? So stimming is when you repeat movements or vocalizations to help to self-soothe."

Amelia smiled broadly. "Petal, that's an excellent way of explaining it to me. So what stims do *you* like?"

"Oh, Mommy, stims are so fun! I likes wiggly stims and also vocal stims. Listen, Mommy!" Mandi made a cooing noise like a dove, and her entire face lit up. "See! Isn't that lovely?"

"It sounds very pretty, darling."

"*And* it feels nice too; in my throat and mouth." More wriggles. "This is fun Mommy, not really a punishment."

"Punishments are not supposed to make you feel bad," said Amelia, "or at least, the punishments I'll dole out aren't meant to do so. They are aimed at helping you regulate, and to learn. So there's no point spanking you as a punishment, because you like it and then I'll end up with a naughty princess all the time, trying to get her spanks!"

"'Xactly," agreed Mandi.

"And the last thing I'd like to teach you before we sort dinner and have our snuggly evening, is square breathing."

"Square breathing?"

Amelia nodded. "It's a really good way of helping you physiologically reset your body. You breathe in for a count of four, hold for four, breathe out for four, and hold for four. And you do *that* four times in a row. Why don't you try it?"

She watched as Mandi closed her eyes and tried, the quiet punctuated only by her slow and steady breathing.

When Mandi was done she opened her eyes and grinned. "How'd I do, Mommy?"

"Excellently, babygirl," said Amelia. "I'm so proud of you." And as her girl leaned in for a cuddle, she realized she really, truly was proud of her girl. And she never want that feeling to leave.

CHAPTER 12

Dinner was a big bowl of pasta, accompanied by some delicious garlic bread. Utterly yummy and, Mandi was pleased to note, perfectly easy to balance on the couch while they watched some television.

"I don't watch television too much," she explained to Mommy Amelia, and so Mommy had picked an episode of *Fraggle Rock* to watch, the one where Wembley tried to please everyone and splits into five different Wembleys.

"Wembley is ver' like me," she said, in between giggles at the Fraggle's antics. "He doesn't like people to be sad or mad, and so he tries to make everyone happy."

"It's lovely to be thoughtful and think about other people," said Mommy, "but not at the expense of yourself, little girl. Princesses need to put themselves first, so that they can protect the kingdom when it needs protecting!"

That had given Mandi food for thought and kept her quiet as she munched her way through her pasta.

She hadn't realized how sleepy she was. And yes, it was partly the excitement of the day—meeting new people, going new places, the incident on the swing—but it was also because the realization of exactly how tired she *always was* had suddenly hit Mandi.

She'd spent the last two years trying to be a grown up for herself and her ex Daddy. She'd had to adjust for his mood swings, for his drinking, and had to prepare herself for the fact she'd never know what was going to happen that day. Everything was always up in the air. Would it be good? Would it be bad? Would she end the day smiling or crying? She never knew and it had worn her out.

And yes, they'd been broken up for a while now, but it didn't feel like her body had caught up to this knowledge yet. It felt as if Mandi was always waiting for the other shoe to drop, probably from a great height, and knock her out.

Utterly exhausting.

And now that she was getting to have a true break, be somewhere completely different, her body was letting her know she needed to sleep. She needed to sleep a lot.

"Mommy," she said, stifling a yawn.

"Yes, darling?"

"I'm really, really tired. Is it okay if we go to bed early?"

"Of course. You're a good girl for telling me. Come on, bathroom time."

Mandi liked the fact that there was no cajoling for her to stay up later, no look of disappointment at how the evening was turning out. Mommy Amelia was actually pleased that Mandi had identified for herself when she needed to go to bed, and her smile had been one of pride.

If Mandi hadn't been so tired, she'd have glowed with happiness, but as it was, it was all she could do to pad into the bathroom after her Mommy.

She watched as Mommy Amelia popped toothpaste onto Mandi's toothbrush and handed it to her. "Here you go, petal."

"T'ank you, Mommy," she said, and focused on brushing her teeth thoroughly.

After she was done, mouth rinsed out, she headed to the bedroom and was about to get undressed when Mommy Amelia stopped her.

"What about your makeup?"

What about her makeup? She looked at the other woman, confused.

"Petal, you can't go to bed with makeup on, it's bad for your skin. Have you got some makeup wipes with you?"

"But I'm too *tired*," she said, a slight whine entering her voice. But when Mommy Amelia raised an eyebrow, she sighed and plodded over to where her makeup wipes where tucked into her bag.

"Bring them here, Mandi dear," said Mommy Amelia.

She did and jumped up to sit where her Mommy patted.

"Turn and face me." She removed Mandi's makeup with deft but firm swipes, and though Mandi didn't usually like the sensation, this time it wasn't too bad. Maybe it was because it was someone else doing it, or maybe it was Mommy Amelia's hand beneath Mandi's chin, holding her face still.

That touch did something to her. Soothed her. It was everything.

"What do you usually wear in bed?"

"I… I… I…" Mandi found herself stuttering, the way she sometimes did when she was Little and was excited about an idea. "I's got Little jammies, if I'm allowed to wear those?"

"Babygirl, you're allowed to wear whatever you like. I know clothes can cause a sensory overload for autistic people, so I'll always let you pick what clothes are going to be best for you."

"Always?" Mandi found herself drooping slightly. She

knew that Mommy was right, but also she'd kind of liked the idea of someone picking out clothes for her to wear.

"Well, if you gave me options that would work for you, I can always pick from those."

Mandi nodded excitedly. "Yes, p'ease!"

"Then we can definitely do that, but tonight I would like you to pick your pajamas out; I want to know what it is you go for when you're beyond tired, darling."

"Okay, Mommy." That made sense, and to be fair, it wasn't as if deciding what to wear in bed that night would take much thinking. Mandi knew exactly what she was going for. Her Lilo and Stitch pajamas.

They were soft, without the usual seams that irritated her skin, and they were so lightweight that if she overheated in the night, it was the easiest thing in the world to kick them off.

"Would you like me to help you undress?"

Mandi nodded sleepily as she handed Mommy the pajamas, her head dropping.

"Arms up!"

It was the first time she was getting undressed in front of her Mommy, and for some reason Mandi didn't feel the slightest bit nervous. Perhaps she should have been, but she was simply far too tired. Clothes off, and the jammies on, and all she had to remind her that Mommy Amelia had seen her naked was a kiss on her tummy before she was being picked up and bounced onto the bed.

"Go on, princess, get your tush up and under the covers. I'll be back in a second."

Mandi crawled up to the top of the bed and got snuggled up, burritoing herself in the blankets until only her face peeked out.

When Mommy returned, a book under one arm, she laughed. "Look at you there; are you all snug?"

She'd also changed into a pinstripe pajama set made of

shiny material that brought to mind the suit she'd worn during the day. Mandi reached out to touch the material and wiggled at how nice it felt. Satin-y.

"Are you coming to bed too, Mommy?"

"Of course, babygirl. I said I was going to stay the night."

"Yes, but it's early and you's a Big."

She laughed. "Bigs need their sleep too, and besides, I've had quite the exciting day. I found myself a Little princess and everything."

That made Mandi beam, and she wriggled over to make room for Mommy, even though there was more than enough room in the king-sized bed.

As soon as Mommy got underneath the blankets and cozied up to Mandi, she popped the book she'd been carrying on top of the covers.

It was a picture book with a colorful cover and the words *Too Much, An Overwhelming Day* printed across the top.

"What's this?" asked Mandi.

"It's a story about a little girl with sensory issues; she doesn't like bright lights or loud noises, and sometimes even people hugging her feels like too much."

"Oh! That's just like me!"

"I know," said Mommy. "I thought you might like it. Oh, babygirl, what's wrong?"

Because Mandi was crying all of a sudden, and it wasn't because she was too tired, and it wasn't because she was sad, it was because she was happy. Because her Mommy had seen her sensory-processing issues and hadn't thought that she was making a fuss, or being silly, or was too much. She had seen that side of Mandi and accepted it without question.

"I…I…" her words staccatoed to a stop.

Then arms were warm around her and she was able to

rest her head on Mommy's chest and cry until she was all out of tears.

When she finally sat up, snuffling, and wiping her eyes with the back of her pajama sleeve, she said, "You like me just as I am."

Mommy Amelia smiled at her. "Of course I do. You are very likeable, just as you are."

"T'ank you." She snuggled up close, slipping her arms around the librarian. "Can you read me the story now."

"I can," and Mommy Amelia opened the book.

CHAPTER 13

When Mandi woke up in the morning, she found that she'd rolled onto her side and somehow become the little spoon to Mommy Amelia's big spoon.

She heard a snuffly snore and giggled quietly. Mommy snored!

Carefully, she extricated herself from the bed, and tiptoed to the bathroom to perform her morning ablutions. But when she got back, Mommy Amelia was looking around blearily-eyed and her gaze fell upon Mandi.

"There you are! I woke and I didn't know where you'd gotten to. Come here, you delicious thing you!"

She tugged at Mandi's hand and Mandi fell on the bed and was vigorously tickled until she was laughing so much she could barely breathe out the word, "Yellow!"

Mommy sat up and looked at her, bemusement written across her face. "I always respect a safeword, little girl; is something the matter, or were you just safewording out because you were scared of being tickled to death?"

Well, that was a challenge Mandi couldn't leave unanswered, and so she launched herself at Mommy, going straight for the sensitive areas behind the knees and under the arms. The gurgle of laughter that spilled over filled her with joy. Hearing Mommy laugh was the best thing ever.

"Oh you…" Then all of a sudden, Mommy slipped one arm behind Mandi's back and flipped her over so that Mommy was on top and Mandi was underneath, and Mandi suddenly started feeling very Big indeed. "Good morning, princess."

"Good morning, Mommy," she said shyly. And then leaned up to press her lips against the other woman's. She swore she experienced a slight chuckle before Mommy Amelia lay her back down and kissed her. Thoroughly.

It was heaven.

It was so heavenly that she almost forgot to breathe, and when they came up for air, she gulped in oxygen.

"Mandi?"

"Yes, Mommy?"

"What would you like to do this morning?"

"I…" she breathed, "I'd like to do…" she let her voice trail off and laughed bashfully. "I mean…"

"Are you saying"—Mommy's mouth was by her ear and she paused in the middle of the sentence to take Mandi's ear between her teeth and nip at it—"you'd like to do *me?*"

The squawk Mandi emitted made them both burst out laughing, and when she had a chance to catch her breath again, Mandi said, "Yes, I suppose I am. If that's okay?"

"Oh, darling," said Mommy, kissing her way down the nape of Mandi's neck. "That is most certainly okay."

When she reached the neckline of Mandi's pajama top, she paused, her pupils wide and dark.

Mandi saw herself reflected there, flushed with longing.

"Can I take this off you, Mandi?"

"Only if you take yours off, Mommy."

And in a movement that echoed the sweet undressing

of the night before, her Mommy tugged Mandi's top up and over her head. But then she sat up, legs straddling Mandi's, and slowly began undoing the buttons of her own top.

Inch by inch, button by button, more of Mommy Amelia was revealed to Mandi at such a slow pace that by the end she was almost raring to tear it off Mommy herself, buttons be damned.

She had the most perfect breasts; small with the prettiest pink nipples that Mandi longed to take in her mouth. "Can I"—she leaned up on her elbows, unable to look away—"please, Mommy. Please, can I…?"

And she loved how Mommy Amelia didn't tease her, didn't make her spell out the words. Because Mommy Amelia knew just what Mandi needed: her.

Pulling Mandi gently forward, she maneuvered her until Mandi was so close that she could kiss her right nipple. And she did. Just a gentle one at first, and then swiping her tongue tentatively across the puckered tip. Mommy moaned, and that was all the encouragement Mandi needed to curl her tongue around the nipple and tug it gently into her mouth so she could suck. She felt desire pooling between her thighs, and she knew that if Mommy touched her there, her fingers would come back wet.

She was vaguely aware of Mommy speaking to her, stroking her hair, cradling her head. "My sweet girl, that's it, just like that." And then when Mommy pulled back, she keened, the noise desperate.

"Now, now, princess. We have all the time in the world. I want to see you. Please?"

Mandi nodded enthusiastically, kicking off her pajama pants until all of her was free, lit by shafts of sunbeams.

Mommy Amelia, sat up then, running her fingers across

every part of Mandi's skin. Over puckered nipples, the expanse of her tummy, dancing across silvery stretch marks. "You are so, so beautiful. My darling, gorgeous girl."

Such frank and honest appraisal made Mandi squirm for a minute, and when she went to cover herself, Mommy Amelia caught her hands, and pulled them up until they were above her head. "No, no, you don't get to hide from me, babygirl." There was a pause, and then she asked tentatively, "Green?"

"Green," Mandi confirmed. In fact, she'd never felt more green. Like her body was a lush wonderland, ready to bloom into life under the watering gaze of this woman —this *goddess*—who looked at Mandi as if she wanted to worship *her*. That wasn't the right way round, Mandi was sure. Surely, she should be worshipping Mommy.

She said as much. "Shouldn't I be pleasing you, Mommy?"

"You are pleasing me, babygirl, all laid out like a veritable snack for me to eat up."

"Yes, but…"

"And yes, you have a delicious butt as well." Mommy Amelia slipped a hand beneath Mandi and squeezed her tush. "So delicious, all for me."

"But, Mommy?" she let some of her anxiety sneak into her voice, and Mommy Amelia stopped joking around and looked at her gently.

"You touching me and doing things to me is going to be delicious and the mere thought of it does things to me, but more than that, I want to treat you. I want to taste you and kiss, and make you come apart in my arms over and over, sweet one. It's been a good while for me; I'm demi and I just haven't particularly wanted to sleep with anyone in a long time. So I know how I experience an orgasm; the joy of being with you is getting to discover what gets you there too. After that, you can play with me. How does that sound?"

Mandi wriggled, hands still pinned, but that didn't keep her from arching up to kiss the other woman. "That sounds perfect, Mommy."

CHAPTER 14

Amelia couldn't get over how Mandi looked laid out beneath her. Her chest was flushed and her more than ample bosoms heaved in a manner that wouldn't be out of place in a romance novel. All soft jiggles.

She looked like she belonged in Amelia's arms. In her bed.

And Amelia was going to show her exactly why she belonged there. She was going to make Mandi come until Mandi couldn't come any more, but before all of that, she was going to taste her.

"I want to taste you, princess. Is that okay?"

The hurried, "Mmhmm," made her chuckle as she kissed her way down the redhead's body. Mandi was so delightfully responsive, as if each of Amelia's touches was a revelation, and a new discovery of pleasure. Trailing fingers down the path her kisses took, made the woman gasp and tense her legs, before relaxing into the sensations.

Amelia wanted to feel Mandi shatter beneath her mouth. *Needed* to feel her shatter. And then she'd take each precious sliver and help piece them back together again.

When she reached Mandi's inner thigh, she paused, waiting, wanting to hear how much Mandi needed her, and she wasn't disappointed.

"Come on!" growled her princess, almost fierce, "what are you waiting for, Mommy?"

"For you to remember your manners, little girl!"

She could almost hear Mandi roll her eyes at her. "You want me to say please?"

Lifting her head, Amelia leaned up and met Mandi's eyes. "Say please like a good girl."

Mandi's lips parted and she blinked hurriedly, fighting the flush that rose in her cheeks. Then the cheekiest smile flitted across her face. "Please like a good girl."

The challenge in her eyes was alight with humor, and Amelia grinned. "Oh like that, is it?"

She lifted her hand and tapped Mandi's clit sharply, the movement a gentle approximation of a slap.

Mandi gasped, and then moaned audibly.

Her little girl had been very honest about what she liked on her entry form, and Amelia intended on fulfilling every single one of her girl's desires.

"Say please."

"Please."

"Please what?"

"Please, Mommy?"

"Please Mommy, what?" She could see the frustrated desire building in Mandi's body, her hips moving upward, desperate for touch.

She was rewarded with a pleading cry. "*Please,* lick me, Mommy!"

"Of course, babygirl," and then she lowered her mouth, and licked from the entrance to Mandi's pussy, all the way up to her clit, swirled around, and sucked the pink nub into her mouth as Mandi's back came off the bed.

"Mommy!" she almost sobbed, and Amelia wished there was a way for her to hold her girl in her arms, kissing her, and licking her all at once. Instead, she reached out to hold Mandi's hands, entwining their fingers together as an anchor.

"I've got you, babygirl," she said, and then licked again.

She'd been born with a tongue-tie, which had never been rectified, so Amelia couldn't extend her tongue very far, just enough to lick and taste Mandi's pussy, so it meant that she really did have to bury her head between Mandi's legs. She kept one nostril free so she could breathe, and then fully lost herself. All she could smell, all she could taste, was her princess.

Loosening her right hand from Mandi's grip, she teased the entrance to her girl's pussy, never quite entering until Mandi said, her voice tight. "Oh for fuck's sake, yes, I want you to finger me, Mommy. Make me take it."

That made Amelia laugh, the vibrations traveling down Mandi's clit and making her cunt clench about Amelia's fingers as they entered her. Two, to begin with. Amelia fingers curled as if beckoning forward in a come-hither motion that she knew would graze up against Mandi's g-spot.

A strangled "Holy fuck," was the result and Amelia was surprised at how foul-mouthed her girl could be. She'd have to put that mouth to good use later, she thought, and then added another finger, to see what curse words her girl might still have in reserve.

Only this time, there was a "Jiminy Cricket!" and Amelia had to concentrate really, really hard not to splutter with laughter right into Mandi's pussy.

She sped up then, sucking and finger fucking and stroking and kissing, and felt Mandi's legs tighten about her head. Tighter and tighter, and then Mandi was crying out, over and over, her pussy clenching and unclenching rapidly around Amelia's fingers as she came.

And before her girl could pause, Amelia leaned up, locked eyes with her, brushed her thumb over Mandi's clit and said, "Come again for me, baby, come for Mommy," and Mandi shattered.

CHAPTER 15

Mandi couldn't think, could barely take in enough breath, she'd come so hard. And when Mommy Amelia clambered up the bed to take her in her arms, she let go of everything and just nuzzled in for cuddles.

"There, there, babygirl," Mommy said. "I've got you. You're all good. Safe with me."

She nodded and then leaned up to kiss her. "I—" She stopped. No matter how much she wanted to, Mandi knew she couldn't say what she was thinking. That it was just sex and the adrenaline rushing through her body. She couldn't have fallen this fast.

She shouldn't fall this fast.

Mommy Amelia sat back and looked at her. "What's going on?"

"It's just, you're amazing. *Amazing*. And sexy and kind and the best Mommy a little girl could ever ask for. But I'm only here for a week. A *week*. And then I have to leave you behind, and I…" Mandi started choking up, and Mommy Amelia looked as distraught as she felt. "I don't know if I'll want to say goodbye."

"Oh, sweetheart, I don't think I'll want to say goodbye either. But you have a world outside the Ranch."

"Do I?" She drew the covers up over her knees. "Sure, I have my own duplex, but I don't have many friends—I let my ex isolate me, which was my own fault—and…"

"Your ex was an abusive—" Mommy Amelia caught herself before she swore. "He wasn't nice to you, and isolating a partner from their friends and family is classic abusive behavior. You're not allowed to blame yourself for that."

Mandi nodded slowly. Logically she knew that was true, but it didn't feel true, not deep down. Deep down she felt like she should have been stronger. Should have challenged him more. Stood up for herself.

Mommy kissed her. "It's okay," she said. "These things take time. But you'll make new friends. You have already done that here."

"I have." Mandi felt wistful. She knew that part of her wished she could be like Sadie and stay here forever. Work in the library, go to bed with Mommy Amelia. Have the life that treated her so harshly stay outside the wrought-iron gates of the Ranch. But life never quite worked out the way that she wanted it to.

She looked at the other woman, brushed ruffled blonde hair from her face. "I'm so glad I met you."

"Oh, darling, me too," said Mommy Amelia. "And I"—she paused, suddenly catching sight of the clock on the wall—"am very late for work! The library opens in half an hour and we're not showered or dressed, and you need to have breakfast!"

"I can do breakfast," said Mandi. "You jump in the shower, I'll prep breakfast, and then I'll run down and join you in the library as soon as I'm showered and ready."

Mommy Amelia leaned over and kissed her deeply.

"You are an absolute star. A treasure. My princess. Thank you!"

She jumped out of bed, shed her pajama pants, and Mandi allowed herself an appreciative look at the other woman's rear end before it disappeared off into the bathroom.

Pottering around the room, she found some granola and yogurt in the fridge, and made up bowls with fresh sliced berries on top, all ready for when Mommy reappeared in the bathroom doorway, a towel wrapped around her body, her short hair still wet.

"Oh, babygirl, this looks amazing. Thank you so much." She pulled Mandi close to her, and kissed her, the scent of coconut enveloping Mandi. It was a nice, refreshing scent that Mandi inhaled deeply. She kissed Mommy Amelia back and smiled.

"Eat up; you don't want to be late!" It felt so nice and cozy; like this was their life, not just one morning of a stolen week together. Mandi's smile became forced, but she tried her utmost to mask and not to let on again. She didn't want to ruin the little time they had left.

Mommy Amelia ate up quickly, put her bowl in the dishwasher, and then kissed her thoroughly, taking Mandi's breath away, before practically running out the door.

Mandi ate her breakfast more slowly and then dragged herself over to the bathroom. She was going to have a shower, because she'd told Mommy she would, but she couldn't have felt less motivated.

And then she stared.

Somehow, as they'd been out and about in the main Ranch, she'd somehow missed seeing the bathroom itself. A large soaking bathtub—big enough for two—stood in one corner, and the other was taken up by one of the largest walk-in showers she'd ever seen. Large and square, with marble walls on two sides, and sheer glass on the other two, it looked like it had a rainfall showerhead!

Mandi couldn't strip quick enough. She turned up the heat until the entire shower was steamed up and then luxuriated under the fall of the water. She closed her eyes, and let the hot water soak into her muscles, loosening the stresses, tensions and worries she'd been carrying, and then washed them all the way down the drain.

Okay, so she might only have six days left, but she wasn't going to waste a single one. She was going to have the best time and savor every second she got to spend with Mommy Amelia.

CHAPTER 16

The Littles' Library was busy that morning. By the time Mandi arrived at work—which was only about half an hour after Mommy Amelia had, once she'd dried her hair—the library was already buzzing with people.

There were two very little Littles, probably Butterflies from the Pre-School program, Mandi guessed, holding hands, and looking through all of the picture books.

"Hello there," she said. "Would you like me to help you pick out some books?"

The two Little girls looked curious. "Who're you?"

"I'm Mandi," she said. "I'm working with Mommy Amelia here in the library this week."

Their eyes grew wide. "Mommy Am—do you mean Miss Grayson?"

"That's right," she said, beaming.

"But, but, she's so *scary*…"

Mandi looked over to where Mommy Amelia was by the library checkout desk and waved. Mommy Amelia waved back and grinned.

The two Littles were awed. "Wooooooow… Miss Grayson knows how to smile?"

Mandi laughed. "Well, she laughs with me. Anyway, what kind of books are you looking for?"

"They were looking for a book to bring to Butterflies this morning," said a voice from behind her. She turned to see Miss Price smiling gently. "Hello, Mandi, you seem to have settled in quite well."

"Yes, thank you," she said, suddenly shy again. Apparently, chatting to other Littles was fine, but talking to Bigs still made her nervous. "I'm doing Big work during the day, working in the Littles' Library, and then I get to be Little the rest of the time."

Miss Price nodded. "That sounds really lovely, and you clearly know what you're doing when it comes to the books. Which one would you recommend for these two? Rachel, Trixie, why don't you tell Mandi what kind of story you'd like to find?"

That question opened multiple floodgates and once she'd waded through the myriad of ideas the two Littles had about the perfect story, she managed to pick out one about unicorns and emotions that seemed like it would suit them both perfectly.

Once they headed off, each of them holding one of Miss Price's hands, she went back to shelving and considered her Little some more.

She'd told Mommy Amelia the previous day that she wanted to encourage her Little to come out more in her day-to-day life, but she didn't know how that was going to gel with working in the library.

Books were wonderful, they helped her feel Little and helped her feel Big and sometimes it was just so confusing about which feeling was which.

Also, books weren't just a Little or Big thing, they also helped Mandi feel more grounded when she was dysregulated. Being autistic meant that sometimes she couldn't control her emotional responses, that they hit her like a huge tidal wave so intensely sometimes she felt like she might drown in them. But books were one of her special interests, and just being around them, running her fingers along book spines, flipping through pages, even the *smell* of books made her feel safe.

Suddenly, she had a brainwave.

"Mommy!" she whisper-shouted as she scuttled over. "Mommy!"

"Yes, petal? How can I help?"

"Would it be okay if I played some music while I worked? I promise I'll take out the earbuds when I'm talking to people, and I won't have the music so loud that it'd disturb anyone, but I think my Little would like it!"

Mommy Amelia beamed at her. "That sounds like an excellent idea; how clever you are!"

She blushed and ducked her head.

"No, no, princess, chin up please."

Slowly, she lifted her chin of her own accord and nodded vigorously several times to encourage herself to remain focused. "Thank you," Mandi said, accepting the compliment, even if it made her insides feel all funny.

"You're welcome. Have you a playlist on your phone you can use?"

"I do! I have one with songs from all my favorite cartoons."

"Well, that sounds perfect," said Mommy Amelia. "Are you going to be focusing on shelving, this morning?"

"Yes, please," said Mandi. "I want to sort out all of our returns, and then I'd maybe like to do one or two different book displays? If that's okay?"

"Brilliant," said her Mommy. "Which ones are you going to focus on?"

"I'd like to do some displays for Mental Health Awareness Month," said Mandi. "I thought I could pull out some picture books for the very Littles, and maybe do a YA selection for the Middles?"

Mommy Amelia looked impressed. "Now that's an excellent idea; I hadn't considered that for this month. Round here we usually focus on Mother's Day in May."

Mother's Day! Mandi had forgotten that holiday was nearly here. And it was this coming Sunday. She instantly knew she wanted to do something extra special for her Mommy Domme. A special Mother's Day for Mommy Amelia.

CHAPTER 17

※

Mandi really was the hardest worker. Once she put her headphones in and switched on her music, she happily zoomed around the library all day. Amelia had to actually remind her to eat lunch!

It was surprising how much had changed in twenty-four hours.

Three days ago, Amelia would have said she was perfectly content to live her life here on the Ranch, working alongside her colleagues, helping Littles find books, art supplies and games that would bring them joy. But now, now she wondered how she'd ever be able to go back to that life without feeling like something was missing.

No. Not some*thing*.

Someone.

She was very happy in her demisexuality, and very happy with her life. But now she'd met Mandi and she didn't even want to begin to imagine what life would be like without her.

It was a sobering thought, and one she decided to

discuss with Derek when, after lunch, things quietened down in the library, and Mandi had said she was more than capable of looking after the space.

"I'll call you if I have any trouble," she said earnestly, and then hurried over to help one of the Middles find a book to read for some homework assignment.

So Amelia found herself wandering down the corridor of the Littles' Wing, toward Derek's office.

"Is he in, Erika?" she asked the dark-haired woman behind the front desk. "I was wondering if he had a moment or two."

"I've always got time for you, Miss Grayson," said Derek's deep voice behind her and she turned and chuckled. "Come on in, Amelia."

They sat down in the two large leather chairs beside his desk.

"So Mandi's certainly been settling in. She told me about your arrangement."

"Yes," said Amelia. "I suppose it's about that… well, that's why I'm here."

Derek nodded for her to continue.

"She's such a sweetheart, and as impossible as it seems, I'm already very, very fond of her."

"That has been apparent to most of us; the staff haven't been able to stop talking about it! Is she okay after her fall yesterday?"

"Oh yes, she's quite all right. Was just overtired, so she had a regulating punishment and then had a very early night."

"Sadie had a regulating punishment too; I imagine our little girls will be quite well behaved this evening for dinner."

Amelia chuckled. "Oh, I bet they will."

"So that all seems excellent; you're both getting along

very well, the new dynamic is working for you... what is it that you're concerned about?"

Amelia took a deep breath. "We've spoken before, Derek, about the way that I am."

"Your demisexuality?"

"My demisexuality. I've never really missed having sex too much, never really found a true connection with any of the Littles or submissives who've come to stay here. But Mandi? She was curled up on that couch in her suite, red hair everywhere, and I just..." She sighed. "It was the connection I didn't know I didn't have. Not instant lust, because that's not the way my brain works, but I did know. I *knew*, Derek, I *knew*."

"And that is bad how?"

"She's leaving! In less than a week! And then I'll have to go back to normal, knowing what my life was like with her in it."

"Perhaps taking a step back then—" The glare Amelia shot him had Derek closing his mouth. Fast.

"I just need you to tell me how to get over someone, so I can prepare for when she's gone."

Derek rolled his eyes. "I swear, the two of you..."

"Wait, what?"

"I think the two of you need to sit down and have a conversation about what it is that you both want. Because maybe it's more than just this week."

Amelia looked up slowly. "I... I can't hold her back. If she wants this experience to help her process the big wide world out there, then I have to let her go."

"That's true," Derek said, his voice quiet, kind. "But I wouldn't assume what she wants. You can't make those decisions for her. You both need to have all of the facts before you can make any big decisions."

She laughed hollowly, "But what can I offer her, Derek?

I have no family, no life on the outside. Just myself, and a home I don't even own."

"If you wanted to own it," he interjected, "we could look into that. And not everyone wants a life on the outside. There are job opportunities here, Caregiving facilities, a school and a university. Just talk to her, Amelia."

Just talk to her. Huh. Maybe that could work…

CHAPTER 18

After work, Mandi went hurrying across the lobby to the Guest Wing. She was so excited at the prospect of cooking dinner for Sadie and Master Derek, that she forgot to put her earplugs in, and actually managed to head across without getting completely overwhelmed.

She even managed a whole conversation with a very overly excited Rachel and Trixie, from Butterflies, who couldn't wait to tell her about how much everyone loved the book she'd recommended. Their Daddies also smiled at her and said they'd like to come by and get some more book recommendations later in the week, and even though they were strange Bigs, she didn't feel scared at all. She could thank book talk for that.

By the time she got back to the room, Mandi was almost elated. She was managing so much, all without having a meltdown. It was wild.

Mommy Amelia had kept her promise and spoken to Chef Connor who ruled the Ranch kitchen, and he'd provided everything Mandi needed to make her favorite mac and cheese. Pancetta and four types of cheese and some broccolini on the side.

Cooking was one of the things that helped Mandi's head switch off, almost completely. It was just her and the recipe. She pulled it up on the reading app on her phone and put on some more music.

The happy wiggles started, and she sang along as she started to measure out all the ingredients.

"Hey, babygirl," said Mommy Amelia. "Need some help?"

"Can you set the table please, Mommy?"

"Of course, lovely."

When a particularly upbeat 80s tune came on, Mandi was delighted to hear Mommy Amelia start humming it, and then she began to sing. Quietly, at first, almost under her breath, and then as the song continued, louder and louder, until she extricated Mandi from the cooking utensils she held and spun her round the kitchen and kissed her.

"Mommy!" she giggled. "I've got to keep stirring!"

"Yeah, yeah." Mommy Amelia waved it off, but still spun Mandi back over to the stove.

Mandi wiggled as she prepped the last bits, before putting all of the mac and cheese in the oven dish and emptying an entire pack of grated mozzarella and cheddar cheese atop it.

"Isn't that a touch too much cheese, petal?"

"But, Mommy," said Mandi, turning large pleading eyes upon Mommy Amelia, "you can't get the cheese pancake without this much cheese."

"The cheese pancake?"

Mandi was horrified. *"You've never had a cheese pancake?"*

"Should I have?"

Mandi bounced up and down on her tiptoes. "Okay, let me just put this in the oven. Right. Cheese pancakes. It's where you put the perfect amount of grated cheese atop anything and bake it in the oven. And then it turns into this layer of the crispiest, most delicious cheese you've ever eaten. It's absolutely heaven."

Mommy Amelia looked unconvinced. "Are you preparing *any* vegetables to go with dinner?"

"Of course! I'm doing tons of steamed broccolini."

"Broccolini?"

"It's the best version of broccoli. Properly yummy, Mommy!"

"That's good then, little girl. I'm proud of you, preparing a delicious meal for your friend and her Daddy, and making sure to include veggies too."

"Thank you, Mommy," Mandi said, but then her face fell. "I forgot dessert! Oh no! I invited them over and didn't even think to—"

"None of that, little girl. I got you," Mommy said, and before Mandi could even start to panic, her Mommy was zooming around the kitchen, pulling together everything she needed to make a delicious dessert.

By the time Sadie and Master Derek knocked on the door to her room, everything was prepped.

Mommy Amelia promised to steam the broccolini, so that Sadie and Mandi could go and chat, and the two of them ran off to bounce on the couch and talk at each other pretty quickly.

Mandi told her new friend all about the new work she'd done in the Littles' Library. "And I got to organize some new book displays for Mental Health Awareness Month!"

"Really? That's amazing!" enthused Sadie. "Are they all picture books?"

"I did different ones for different Littles. Some for the Caterpillars and Butterflies, some for the older Littles and some for the Middles. I wanted to make sure that everyone was included. Looking after your mental health is super important."

Sadie nodded, looking serious for a moment. "When I came here, things had been… difficult for me. We have some really great counselors on the Ranch though."

"Yes, Master Derek said so. I've got my first appointment with Catherine Denten tomorrow. I'm a little bit nervous though."

Sadie gave her a hug. "It's normal to be nervous. Do you have a counselor at home?"

Mandi shook her head. "It wasn't covered by my health insurance, and that was before the bookshop I worked in closed. So I'm going to take full advantage while I'm here and I can." She looked wistful. "I really wish I didn't have to leave, Sadie. The world out there? It really wasn't kind to me. And I never felt… well, right."

"I hate that, when you know you just don't fit in."

"I don't really have it here," explained Mandi. "Maybe it's because I feel like I belong, but I also get the feeling that standing out also isn't a bad thing."

"It definitely isn't!" said Sadie. "Although sometimes it might feel that way when you're standing out because of a prank."

The timer went off just then, and the two Littles jumped up.

"Dinner!" yelled Sadie.

"Coming through!" yelled Mandi, the loudest she'd been since she'd arrived and they both burst into fits of giggles.

"I think," said Mommy Amelia, "that it might be a good idea if *I* get the food out of the oven?"

"I agree," said Master Derek, but the two Bigs didn't look like they were cross at all. In fact, they looked really happy.

Mandi did a small happy wiggle. This was exactly what she'd wanted. Good food for her new friends. And for her Mommy.

She looked over at where Mommy Amelia was dishing up the food, and their eyes met.

"You were right about the cheese pancake," said Mommy Amelia. "It looks delicious."

And Mandi felt so accepted and happy that she did the biggest wiggle she'd ever done.

Dessert was rice pudding, all thick and creamy and delicious—despite Sadie's assertion that rice didn't belong in puddings—and Mommy Amelia even put a dollop of jam on Mandi's helping, because she'd been so very good and well behaved that day.

But before she could get too tired, Master Derek and Sadie headed off, and Mommy Amelia helped her rinse the dishes and put them in the dishwasher.

But when the idea of bedtime was raised, Mandi protested. "I'm not even tired yet!" she said. "And yesterday I was in bed *suuuuuper* early."

"Is that so?" asked Mommy Amelia.

"It is so," said Mandi stubbornly. And then added, just in case, "I don't think I'm being rude, Mommy, but I'm really just not all that tired yet."

"Perhaps," said Mommy Amelia, "we could do something else instead?"

"Ooooo… like what?"

"Well, on your entry form, you said that you really liked floggers, so I brought some of mine from home. Would you like to have a look at them?"

Would Mandi? She almost trembled with excitement. "Yes, please, please, please, Mommy!"

Mommy Amelia laughed. "Okay, let me get my bag."

Her bag was truly a bag of wonders, and Mommy Amelia took out each flogger and laid it out on the bed for them both to look at.

There were all sorts, different lengths and weights and materials. There was even one weird looking one, that when Mandi picked it up, Mommy Amelia explained was made from the inside of bicycle tires.

"What?"

"I had a bicycle crash, a good long while ago, and didn't want it to go to waste. I used the frame to make a shoe rack!"

Mandi giggled, and hurriedly put it down and picked up the next.

Her favorite, though, was a super-soft suede flogger, a midweight with plenty of heft behind it. It had looked a little intimidating when she'd first seen it, all black, unlike some of the prettier, rainbow and pastel colored floggers on the bed, but when she picked it up, her Mommy's eyes softened slightly, and Mandi suspected that this might be her Big's favorite.

Mommy Amelia encouraged her to try it out on her own arm, so she could see what it felt like.

It felt… right.

"This please," Mandi said. "Would you mind if we used this one, Mommy?"

Mommy Amelia leaned over and kissed her. "I wouldn't mind whatsoever. Come on, petal, up you get."

Mandi bounced up and looked excitedly toward her Mommy. "How would you like me?"

"On all fours, your tush up in the air. You think you can do that?"

Mandi wriggled in excitement. "Yes, yes, yes! I can do that, Mommy."

She shed clothes quicker than she'd ever shed clothes before, and clambered onto the bed, up on all fours, and unabashedly waved her bottom. "I'm ready, Mommy!"

Nothing happened at first, Mandi was left to feel the air cool against her tush, and the sensation of it made her give a tiny wiggle.

Mommy Amelia ran her hand over Mandi's backside,

and those sensations went shivering up Mandi's spine, and all the way down to her core. "Let's go through a few ground rules first, yes?"

"But, *Mommy*…"

Mommy Amelia didn't say anything, just waited patiently, and Mandi gave up complaining, and said "Yes, Mommy," just as she was supposed to.

"We're using traffic lights?"

"Yes, please: green; yellow; and red."

"And what do those mean for you?"

"Green is go, go, go; yellow means pause for a breather; red means stop and check in with me."

"Not stop altogether?"

Mandi wriggled, but slightly awkwardly. "I have C-PTSD, Mommy, so sometimes something can trigger me and it only needs a slight adjustment, as opposed to a complete end to the scene. If that makes sense?"

Mommy Amelia knew exactly what C-PTSD was—complex post-traumatic stress disorder—and she knew what it meant. Her little girl had experienced ongoing trauma and abuse, rather than a single significant traumatic event, and so her trauma responses could vary in intensity and how they manifested. If she had anything to do about it, she was going to make sure Mandi felt protected and safe when they played. To look after her, the way that she always should have been. Leaning forward, Amelia kissed Mandi's shoulder. "It makes perfect sense. Thank you for explaining for me. You're such a good girl."

Those two words felt comforting, and Mandi let them seep into her body, warming every inch of her.

"Thank you, Mommy."

Mommy Amelia's hand massaged her tush and Mandi purred loudly. "You're an excellent girl, and I'm going to flog you today because of that. You deserve to feel good, babygirl, and I know that this will make you feel good."

It would, and it had been far too long since Mandi had felt the seductive pull of subspace.

"Are you ready, babygirl?"

"Yes, Mommy," said Mandi. "Completely green here."

CHAPTER 19

The first kiss of the flogger against Mandi's tush made her gasp… and then laugh.

Pure joy came tumbling out of her. That one strike felt like absolutely everything she'd ever needed. It felt like a kiss, a caress, a love letter, all wrapped up in one.

And more than anything else, it quieted her brain.

Her brain was always on, always going, whether that was with anxiety, work or getting all excited about her special interests. But it was exhausting. Tiring.

Mandi was done with overthinking.

Well, maybe not entirely done with overthinking, but in this moment, she couldn't overthink.

Not wasn't overthinking.

Couldn't overthink.

The sensations of the flogger, the contrast between the soft suppleness of the suede, and the thudding sting of the impact, it all drew her attention to one focused point.

Her physicality.

She couldn't overthink because she couldn't think. She could only feel.

The second strike made her laugh again, and then they fell with varying rhythms and patterns, and she went floating off into the calm delights of subspace. It helped that she couldn't predict the next strike, when or where it would fall, because it meant that she couldn't do anything but give herself over to the sensations.

Her subspace was calm, quiet—despite the sound of the flogger that she technically knew was still there.

Mommy Amelia checked in with her regularly, asking if she was green, occasionally pausing to trace the marks her flogger left behind with her fingers. That made Mandi shudder almost as much as the thud of the suede.

"You're such a good girl," said Mommy Amelia, "taking all of Mommy's flogs."

Mandi giggled, feeling almost drunk on the sensations. "More please, Mommy."

"More?"

"Harder. Please, Mommy."

Mommy Amelia chuckled softly. "You really do like flogs, don't you?"

Giggling spacily, Mandi nodded, which was slightly difficult from her position on all fours, face pressed into the coverlet. "Yes, yes I do!"

"Okay then, here they come!" And Mommy Amelia increased the intensity and speed. It wasn't too fast; it was the ideal speed, allowing Mandi to adjust to the sensations without having to safeword.

At some point, Mandi wasn't entirely certain when the flogging transcended into an out-of-body experience. She was aware of the impact of the strikes, could feel them warming her tush, could feel the laughter bubbling up and the moans that escaped as she got wetter and wetter. But, at the same time, it felt unreal. Like she was floating over her body, watching herself revel in the whole experience.

Freed from the confines of her body. No longer locked in a physical state that brought with it so much overwhelm and distress.

Free.

And then she started to cry. Quietly at first, and then more and more, until she could taste the salt on her lips.

She became vaguely aware of the flogs ceasing, of Mommy Amelia placing the flogger on the bed beside her, and then rolling Mandi onto her side and pulling her in close to soothe her.

"It's okay, babygirl. I've got you. Let it all out."

Mandi wasn't entirely certain what she was crying over. Perhaps it was the release of emotion, the build-up of having to be on, having to be perfect every day *out there*; perhaps it was grief for this side of herself that she'd thought she'd lost.

Perhaps it was simply because for the first time in forever, she felt so looked after, so cherished, so *loved*, when she'd really managed to convince herself that she wasn't loveable. Not as she was.

All her life, people had thought she was weird, "quirky," too emotional, too enthusiastic, too much.

She hated being too much. Hated this world that punished her for it. Punished her for being neurodiverse in a world designed for neurotypical people. Because for her being neurodiverse meant being hyper-sensitive—to emotions, to sounds, to space. It meant being the odd one out—always. It meant never really belonging.

And the world had told her this for so long, at school, at work, at home, that she'd started to believe it. Her ex had told her that the day they'd broken up. "You're too much," he'd said. "You're too much all of the time." And she'd believed him.

Mandi sobbed harder.

It was only now, here in this moment, she realized she wasn't too much.

The world just hadn't been *enough* for her.

She shuffled, turned just a smidgeon too quickly to face Mommy Amelia that her boob hit her in the face. It made them both giggle.

"I'm not too much." It wasn't a question. It was a statement.

"You're not."

And then she kissed Mommy Amelia. Put all her longing and caring and gratitude into that one movement, running her hands through short shorn hair.

"Please," she said, "please, may I taste you, Mommy?"

Mommy Amelia seemed to realize how important this was to her, because she kissed Mandi back so sweetly, cupping Mandi's face in her hands. "Yes, darling girl, of course you may."

She moved down the bed, throwing aside all attempts at being graceful or sexy; she just needed Mommy. Needed Mommy to feel as good as she did, needed Mommy to be overcome with pleasure.

A hand reached out and held hers. "You'll hold my hand, babygirl?"

The open vulnerability on her Mommy's face moved Mandi. "Always, Mommy," she said.

Taking Mommy's trousers off took some doing, and then her unadorned boxers beneath might have felt plain on any other woman, but on Mommy they looked perfect.

Perfect and wet.

Mandi could see Mommy's desire painting the seams, dark fabric turning darker, and she tugged at the waistband. "May I, Mommy? Please?"

Mommy Amelia was blushing, she could see. "Yes, Mandi, petal. Yes, please touch Mommy."

When she ran her finger up from Mommy's opening to her clit, it came back slick.

"Oh," she breathed. "You're so wet."

"That's because of you, darling." Mommy's words sounded strained, and Mandi looked up, worried.

"Are you okay, Mommy? Do you need to yellow?"

"Maybe just for a second," said Mommy Amelia. "I think I need to explain something."

CHAPTER 20

AMELIA WAS TORN, oscillating between overwhelming desire, and all-consuming fear. She wanted the touch of Mandi's tongue, wanted it so much that she could barely think straight (although thinking *straight* wasn't something she'd done since she'd come out at the ripe old age of nine), but she knew that she needed to explain about her sexuality. About her demisexuality.

"Babygirl," she said, and Mandi clumsily clambered back up to curl up in her arms. "I know I explained before that I'm demi, but I just wanted you to know what that means for me; because it's different for everyone."

"That makes sense," said Mandi, and kissed her so unabashedly that Amelia wanted to melt into her Little girl's arms and never let go.

"For me, it means I don't usually feel much sexual attraction, and never for strangers. I need a connection with someone to feel attracted to them. I can enjoy sex without sexual attraction, but then it's more the actions that are getting me off than the person I'm with, if that makes sense."

Mandi nodded slowly.

"What I'm saying is that me being wet like this…" Damn this felt vulnerable; she found herself wanting to duck her head, the way that she'd seen shy Littles, and the shy Little presently in her arms, do. "Well, it's because we have a connection. And that's not a small thing for me. It means something. I'm not saying we have to label things or decide what that means for us, right now, or even this week, I'm just saying that I care deeply for you, and that's why you affect me like this."

There was a prolonged pause, and Amelia found herself wanting to bury her face under the covers, to hide away from whatever Mandi's response would be.

Instead, she felt soft lips press against her cheek in a kiss.

"I think," said Mandi, "I feel that connection too. Deeply. And it means something to me as well. Maybe tomorrow, once I've done my counseling session, we can sit down and have a chat about what we think this connection means?"

The relief that washed over Amelia was all-encompassing. "Yes, I'd really like that."

"Now," said Mandi, a wicked smile creeping across her features, "if it's okay, I'd like to go back to touching your pussy, Mommy."

Amelia had to bite back a moan. "I suppose… I suppose that would be okay."

"You suppose?" Mandi's smile was teasing. "Only suppose?"

"Oh, you cheeky little thing; go on, touch me like a good girl."

One second Mandi was in her arms, and the next she was scrambling down the bed so that she could sit between Amelia's legs. There was nothing smooth or sophisticated about her enthusiasm, and that only made Amelia want her more. Her complete lack of self-consciousness, the wholeheartedness of her attention, it was utterly enchanting.

She began to laugh as Mandi furrowed her brow and focused in on her pussy. It was like being inspected by the most adorable thing ever.

But then when Mandi ran gentle fingers up the insides of Amelia's thighs, she let out a sigh and allowed herself to relax into the sensations.

Fingers were followed by lips, and the tiniest kisses peppered her legs, all leading up to where her clit waited, almost trembling in anticipation. She couldn't think. Couldn't do anything but wait, angling her hips up in the hope that Mandi would kiss her sooner.

Mandi's left hand reached out for Amelia's and once they connected, gave her Mommy's hand a squeeze. "I got you, Mommy," she said right before she dipped her head lower and licked.

Her tongue was soft and warm and knew exactly where to focus its attentions. Flicking over Amelia's clit, and then circling round, and then in one glorious movement, Mandi sucked the plump clit into her mouth and Amelia thought she was going to come apart right there.

She looked down at where Mandi's red hair fanned out across her belly and moaned. The sight took her breath. It was so beautiful, the reddish gold strands a vivid contrast against her skin. She reached down and stroked the fiery strands that covered her body, running the silken tresses through her fingers.

I love you, she felt herself thinking, immediately strangling the thought so it couldn't be vocalized. But it didn't do any good because she did. She knew it in her very soul. She knew that all she wanted was to worship this girl and be worshipped in return.

Mandi lifted her head, gray eyes peeking up from

between Amelia's legs. "How'd you feel about fingers?" she asked.

"In general?" asked Amelia, teasingly and then gasped as Mandi sucked on her clit and then flicked it back and forth with her tongue intensely. "Fine, fine, I would very much like to feel your fingers in me, princess."

"That's better, Mommy," said Mandi, a mischievous glint in those beautiful gray eyes. "You've got to use your words."

"Why, you little—" but whatever it was Amelia had been about to say was cut off as Mandi slid one—no, two—fingers inside her. Amelia screwed her eyes shut and just breathed, trying her hardest not to come on the spot.

She was always very good at making herself orgasm, efficient, one might say, but it was nothing compared to her princess between her legs, fully focused on bringing her pleasure.

Amelia didn't want to rush it, wanted to let everything build so that she could shatter. It had been way too long since she'd been able to draw on a connection like this during sex, and she didn't want to waste a moment.

Mandi's fingers moved inside her, curling forwards, brushing up against her g-spot and Amelia swore then, her sight whiting out momentarily as she orgasmed with a power she'd never experienced before. Her pussy clutched at Mandi's fingers, the pressure about her clit so intense that Amelia threw her head back and shouted out her pleasure to the ceiling.

She was too sensitive after that for more, tapping out on Mandi's shoulder until her girl, mouth glistening with Amelia's pleasure, lifted off her pussy and smiled up at her.

"Are you okay, Mommy?" Mandi asked.

Was she okay? Amelia wasn't sure. She felt wrung out.

"Yes, babygirl," she said. "Come here."

And even though she'd had every intention of wringing pleasure from Mandi until her girl couldn't come anymore, they fell asleep in each other's arms almost instantly.

CHAPTER 21

Waiting to see Dr. Denten the next morning was very nerve-wracking.

Mandi sat on the bench outside the psychologist's office and tapped her foot incessantly, the sound echoing against the white marble floor.

She'd woken up in Mommy Amelia's arms this morning, and it had been lovely. This time they'd remembered about work and had gotten up with plenty of time to have breakfast together and head downstairs. Mandi had gotten on with her displays, until a quarter to eleven had hit and Mommy had suggested that she go a bit early so she wouldn't be late.

In hindsight, all that had meant was that Mandi had spent the last fifteen minutes sitting outside Dr. Denten's office, working herself up into a bit of a tizzy. By the time the psychologist opened the door, Mandi was wriggling in a decidedly unhappy manner.

"Hello, Mandi, I'm Catherine Denten, or as the Littles call me, Ms. Cat. However, if you'd like, when in our sessions, you may call me Cat," she said, short brown hair falling in front of her face. "Would you like to come in?"

"Not really," said Mandi, and forced a smile. "But I guess that's the point with something like this, right? If we wanted to do it, then we wouldn't have to."

"Well," said Dr. Denten, "sometimes working on ourselves becomes something that we actually enjoy doing, even if it's tough at times."

Mandi nodded stiffly, stood and walked into the room. She knew she was behaving weirdly, but she had no way of moderating her actions at this point, she was so overwhelmed.

"Mandi, why don't you take a look around before we settle into the session?" said Cat. "There's no rush. I've got an hour penciled in for us to talk."

An hour felt like a very long time. "Sure," said Mandi, and she headed straight for the bookshelf. There were books, games and some toys there, but no stuffies. She browsed the books for a bit, tapping her foot and jiggling around to try and get all of her nerves out.

"Would you like to do a big yell?" asked Cat. "Sometimes that can help us to settle our nervous systems. The part of your brain that contains your amygdala is responsible for your fight or flight instincts and often triggers anxiety and panic attacks. We're so used to stress being a part of our day to day lives, that our brains never fully have the chance to reset. Our brains are permanently afraid that we're about to get eaten by a tiger!"

The visual her words caused to instantly appear made Mandi giggle. "So you're saying I should shout to scare away the tiger?"

"It's one of the things you can do to help reset your body physiologically. Would you like to give it a go?"

Mandi nodded, but her first attempt was more of a little quiet, "Argh."

"Argh? Is that it?" Cat sat in one of oversized chairs near the coffee table. "Why don't you try that again, and this time you make yourself as big as you can possibly get. Stretch *all* the way out and yell. And it doesn't have to be 'argh', it can be any word or noise you like."

Mandi turned to face the window, solidly planted her feet shoulder's width apart, and let loose. There weren't any distinguishable words, or even a noise that could be described in a single syllable, but it felt as if her pain had been wrenched from the very depths of her soul, and when she was done, she stood there, panting heavily.

"Now, *that* was an excellent noise," said Cat Denten. "Would you like to talk now?"

Mandi nodded. "Do I have to sit on a chair?"

"Not at all; you can sit wherever you like. And there's a purple stuffie called Ellie behind the couch, if you'd like to cuddle him?"

A stuffie seemed like an excellent idea, and Mandi internally berated herself for not thinking to bring along Beau.

"I have a stuffie," she said. "His name is Beau but I left him in my room 'cause I'm stupid."

"Well, that's a very harsh word to use about yourself," said Cat. "Why don't you grab Ellie and come sit down and tell me why you feel that way."

Ellie was an excellent stuffie, a huge purple floppy thing that fit in Mandi's arms perfectly. It felt like his trunk was hugging her.

She flopped onto the floor and looked up at Cat. "'Cause I know he makes me feel better, but I forgot to bring him anyways." Shifting, she realized that her Little was peeking out. "I's gone a little bit Little, is that okay?"

"Of course it is," said Cat. "I know a lot of Littles. Hello, Little Mandi."

"Hello," Mandi muttered back and fought the urge to suck her thumb.

"So why are you here?"

"'Cause I'm scared, like, all of the time. And Master Derek said if I wanted to stay, then talking to someone would be a good idea, and so I'm doin' the talkin'." She was dropping letters all over the place, her anxiety coming through in her words. "But also, I almost lost my Little 'cause I had a horrible Daddy. I didn't want to be Little anymore 'cause I was doing it wrong."

"I don't think," said Cat gently, "that it's even possible to do being Little wrong."

That stopped Mandi's torrent of words and she furrowed her brow, thinking hard. "No?"

"Well, I've met all kinds of Littles, both here on the Ranch and out there in the big wide world. And all of them are unique; being Little means something different to everyone. I'm always somewhat envious of Littles myself— in therapy we are always encouraging people to heal their inner child, and you Littles seem to have a shortcut to that inner child built in!"

Mandi smiled shyly. It was nice to hear someone see being Little as something other than just a kink. The kinky aspect of it was fun, but it was more to her than that. So much more. "This is true," she said. "I suppose that's kind of lucky."

"What do you think it is that your Little is trying to heal?"

Mandi didn't have to think too hard; she knew immediately. "My Little wants me to be happy. I think she went away for a while because I didn't know if I could ever be happy again, and I didn't want her to be infected by that. Didn't want her to be sad."

"It's okay for Littles to be sad sometimes, did you know that?"

Mandi shook her head furiously. "No!"

"No?" Cat didn't seem cross, just curious.

"No, I'm supposed to look after her, and if she's sad,

then I'm not looking after her properly." She sobered up, suddenly Big. "If she's super sad, then I'm not looking after *me* properly."

That felt somewhat like a breakthrough.

"I guess," she continued slowly, "I guess it felt like it was okay for me to be sad, as long as my Little side didn't feel sad too. If she's really, really sad, then it feels like I'm properly broken." Her eyes started to well up. "I don't want to be broken."

She hugged Ellie the Elephant to her and rocked back and forth where she sat, letting her tears soak the stuffie's fur.

Cat didn't say much, just pushed a box of tissues toward her on the table. It was nice actually, not having someone interject or step in or try and push her into pretending she was all right when she wasn't. Mandi suddenly felt as if it was okay *not to be okay*. She'd never had that sensation before.

"In what ways do you think you're broken, Mandi?"

"Logically I know that all the ways I think I'm broken aren't actually things. But I still feel them."

"Well, tell me what you feel."

"I feel like I'm too much. That being autistic means that I'm never going to fit in or belong anywhere. That I do things *wrong* because I don't know the rules, or the ways that I'm supposed to do them. And that's *hard*. It's exhausting to have to guess and second guess every decision you make, every action you take. I hate it."

Cat looked sympathetic. "That does sound hard. Really hard."

Mandi sighed. "It is, and out there, in the world?" She gestured toward the window. "Out there, people care if you're different. They don't like it. If you don't fit in, then you're cast out and I hate that about it."

"You say 'out there'; does it mean that it feels different 'in here'?"

Mandi nodded. "It does. In here, I feel like I actually belong, like I don't have to squeeze myself into a tiny box to make myself fit in."

"Have you considered staying here for longer?"

Mandi sighed. "I can't really afford it."

"I'm not saying stay here as a guest, I mean stay here as a Little. Master Derek said that you've been working in the Littles' Library, and he has been looking to hire an assistant librarian to help Amelia Grayson. There are options if you want to explore them."

Frozen.

That's how Mandi felt.

Frozen solid.

"Mandi? Are you okay?"

"I… I… I don't know how I could do that."

"What do you mean?"

"I've been"—she blushed hotly—"trying out a dynamic with Momm-Amelia Grayson. It's been amazing. Best thing ever, but this is my third day. There's u-hauling, and then there's *u-hauling*."

That made Cat laugh. "It doesn't mean that you'd have to move in with Amelia; you could continue on with developing your relationship—if the both of you wanted—at a pace that suited you best. You could room in the Littles' Wing instead. You might find it helpful for making friends, actually."

"But wouldn't that put pressure on her, to continue this?"

Cat looked thoughtful. "If you like, we could brainstorm how best you could bring up this idea with her, so as not to pressure her into continuing the dynamic if it's not something she wants long-term. I'm not saying—" she added hurriedly, looking at Mandi's trembling lip, "that she's not looking for something long term, but that's a conversation you'd have to have with her. And you'd need to speak with Master Derek as well, of course."

Mandi nodded, thoughtfully. "And if I did, would it be possible to continue seeing you? Maybe some regular sessions?"

"Definitely," said Cat.

She knew that such huge changes deserved consideration, but Mandi felt as if a weight had been lifted off her shoulders. For the first time in a long time, she had hope.

CHAPTER 22

After the session, Mandi headed back to her room to think things through. Ms. Cat had been so lovely, but the whole experience had raised so many questions for her about what she wanted to do and who she wanted to be.

Mommy Amelia had suggested she might need some processing and decompression time after therapy, so she shot off a quick text to let her know that it went well, and to explain that she was going to maybe have a bath and relax.

But when she went to put her phone down, it rang. It was her cousin, Ralphie, calling.

"Hey, cuz!" he said, his tone buoyant. "How're you finding the Ranch?"

Popping the phone on loudspeaker, Mandi slipped her shoes off and clambered under the bed covers, pulling the blankets up tight around her. "Hey, Ralphie, it's… good."

"Just good? That sounds concerning. Is it not going the way you wanted it to?"

"No, no," she reassured him, "Everyone here is lovely! I just had a counseling session, and it was a whole lot."

There was a pause on the other end of the phone. "Counseling? I didn't know they offered that."

"Yes, they have two psychologists on staff, fully qualified, and Master Derek suggested that it would be a good idea for me to see one. The taxicab driver was a bit mean when I arrived and I got a little upset and..." Her voice trailed off. "But it's okay, because the staff here dealt with it amazingly, and set me up with Dr. Denten."

"That sounds really positive, Mandi," he said. "And how about the rest of it? Are you doing lots of fun things?" She could almost hear him waggle his eyebrows, and in the background heard his fiancé Nate say, "Honestly, Ralphie, let your cousin have some privacy."

She giggled. "Well actually, I might have met someone."

"You have? Who? Tell me *everything!*"

"Her name's Amelia Grayson and she's the head librarian for the Littles' Library, here on the Ranch."

"Oh yeah? Is she all prim and proper?"

"Some of the other Littles think she's a bit intimidating, but *I* think she's lovely."

"Proper Mommy Domme vibes, eh?"

Mandi blushed and her answering silence told Ralphie everything he needed to know.

"*You've found a Mommy Domme!* Mandi, that's *amazing*!" But then, once he'd taken a breath, Ralphie realized the thing that had also been bothering Mandi. "But you're only there for a week—"

"I've been thinking about that," she cut in. "Ralphie, do you think it would be weird if I stayed?"

His voice sounded serious when he answered. "You've only known her for three days, Mandi sweetheart. I'm not sure that changing your life for someone—"

"It wouldn't be for her," Mandi explained. "It'd be for me. Sure, I'd like to keep seeing where this relationship goes, but more than that, I feel like I belong here. The outside world is so big and overwhelming for me; so loud, and so unaccommodating. And my one bastion of safety—the bookshop—is closing, so I'll have to find a new job anyways. I've been working as an assistant librarian here, and… and… and…" She ran out of steam.

"It sounds like you've been really unhappy," he said gently.

"I have," she said. "And not just because of my ex."

"Your super-shitty ex," he corrected.

"Yes, my super-stinky ex," she agreed, switching out the curse word for one that she knew Mommy Amelia would approve of. "You know what it's like, being neurodiverse in a world that's not built for us."

"Yes, I really do. And it's not like either of us had the best family around to support us."

She shook her head in agreement, and then repeated it again so that he could hear. "No, we didn't." Ralphie's parents had disowned him when he'd come out, and his grandfather (not hers) had taken him in. And while Mandi's parents hadn't been openly homophobic, they certainly hadn't understood her. After she'd gone to college and moved out, she'd managed to drift out of their lives without some big blow up.

"So you wouldn't move in with Amelia, is it?"

"Yes, and no, I don't think so. I still need to talk to her about it, and to Master Derek, but if it's an option, I'm seriously considering it."

"Look," said Ralphie, and Mandi didn't know when she'd ever heard him be so serious for a prolonged amount of time. "Life is too short to be unhappy. I think you should go for it; maybe do a trial run, see how it goes, and don't sell your duplex until you're certain."

"That… that could work," Mandi agreed. "Thank you, Ralphie. And you'd come and visit?"

"Of *course* Nate and I will come and visit!" said Ralphie, "I wanna check out that Dungeon!"

Hearing Nate groaning and whisper-shouting that stuff was *private,* Mandi giggled and said goodbye, not completely sure her cousin actually even heard her.

CHAPTER 23

Mandi was all curled up in bed when Amelia got up to her room after work.

"Hey, babygirl," she said. "How are you doing? Want a cuddle?"

"Yes, please, Mommy," she said, big gray eyes pleading.

Jumping up onto the bed, Amelia pulled Mandi toward her and smiled as the redhead nestled in close. "Sounds like you had a big afternoon."

Mandi nodded vigorously.

"Want a quiet evening, just us?"

"Yes, p'ease," mumbled her Little girl, and snuggled up closer. "I's tired, Mommy."

"You are tired, aren't you? Do you want to talk about it?"

Her snuggle monster nodded, face still cozied up. "Can we eat first? There's leftover mac & cheese in the fridge, and we can have veggies with them? An' an' an', can we eats them on the couch?"

"That seems like an excellent idea, babygirl," said Amelia as she extracted herself from a very clingy Mandi and went off to sort out dinner.

It was nice actually, cooking for someone else, for once. She'd gotten so used to prepping food for herself that it had become fuel, instead of pleasure. But seeing Mandi's happy food wriggles inspired her some; and she found herself cutting slices of zucchini, eggplant and peppers into hearts, before roasting them; putting the offcuts into a container in the fridge, to use as the base for a pasta sauce the following day.

When it came to time to eat, Mandi shuffled over to the couch, the entire coverlet still wrapped round her, like an oversized cloak.

But the delight in her voice when she saw the heart-shaped vegetables on her plate made Amelia's in her chest soar. "Mommy! You made me heart veggies!"

"I did, petal. Now eat up before it gets cold."

Amelia set the television to watch the next episode of *Fraggle Rock*, and the two of them tucked in, Amelia pausing every now and then to remind Mandi to drink some water.

"You like water an awful lot, Mommy," said Mandi. "Is it your favorite?"

That made her chuckle, because if she was being honest, she was terrible at making sure she drank enough water herself. "Not my favorite, but I know that it's good for me, so I make sure I have some." She made a mental note to up the size of her water bottle and another to go to the Ranch store and see about finding a cute water bottle for her Little girl.

Mandi seemed so content, watching all the Fraggles work together to solve each other's problems, that Amelia really didn't want to ruin it by asking her about therapy, but when they'd finished dinner, and the third episode came to a close, Mandi brought it up herself.

"Hey, Mommy?"

"Yes, petal?"

"Can we have that talk now?"

"Of course we can." Amelia paused, unsure where to start.

Mandi was all Big Mandi now, letting the blanket slide down from around her shoulders. "It's okay, I know what I want to say, I think."

"Go right ahead."

She paused, and Amelia realized that her girl was nervous, so she reached out a hand and squeezed Mandi's. "You've got this."

Mandi squeezed back, and then took her hands and placed them tightly under her arms, almost like a cage. But as she spoke, Amelia realized that it wasn't a cage at all, it was protection.

"So I think it might have come across a few times that I sometimes find it difficult, 'out there'." She made quotation marks with her fingers. "Partly because of how anxious I get, and partly because of my autism. People haven't always been very kind to me—they aren't when you don't fit in. But the thing is that I'm not inherently broken, not really, and this is one of the first places I've ever been where I've truly felt other people believed that too. You've all—and especially you, Amelia—just accepted me for who I am."

Amelia felt a twinge at hearing her name without Mommy prefixing it, but it emphasized how serious a topic this was to Mandi, so she nodded and listened.

"I like it here. A lot. I feel safe and happy, and people like me. I even feel like I might be able to get know other people. Not everyone all at once, but bit by bit." She took a deep breath and dove into the next sentence. "I guess what I'm saying is that I'm thinking about asking Master Derek about possibly staying. But I don't want you to feel overwhelmed or pressured or any of that. Getting to know you has been"—and here she blushed, pink painting even the tips of her ears—"one of the best experiences, but I know you weren't expecting this. And if I did stay, we could continue on, or not, as you choose. It's not a u-hauling situation; I'd stay in the Littles' Wing, and we'd get to know each other better. Keep on as we are."

She met Amelia's eyes, her gray eyes earnest as if trying to express how serious she felt about what she was saying. "I don't want to freak you out, and this isn't me attempting to push what we have into a different stratosphere, but this place is special. I feel safe here, and if you're comfortable with it, I'd like to explore what that might look like for me."

Those were a whole lot of words in one go, and Amelia needed a moment to consider how she felt. "You did an amazing job of explaining how you feel, baby. Give me a moment to process it. I'm not," she added hurriedly, "stressed or cross; I just want to make sure I address all the things you said."

"That's okay," said Mandi. "How about I pop to the bathroom, and we can talk about it when I'm back?"

She looked nervous though, and Amelia caught her hand before Mandi could slip into the bathroom. "Thank you, for sharing with me. And I know we can definitely work it all out. I just want to make sure I don't give you a glib, quick answer, but really think through what I say."

Mandi nodded, and when she went into the bathroom, Amelia let out the breath she'd been holding.

All she'd been able to think about today was Mandi. She'd even almost missed two prankster Butterflies attempting to sneak out some of the Middle books. Luckily, she'd averted that disaster and sent them to talk to Miss Price.

This connection she had with Mandi had completely bowled her over, almost upended her life and she'd been meaning to talk to her about what it might mean when

Mandi left; if she'd consider a long-distance relationship of some sort, perhaps. But the idea that Mandi might stay…

Well, it was an idea that Amelia could get fully on board with.

"Amelia?" the voice at the bathroom door was shy, and she beamed at her girl as Mandi peeked around the doorjamb.

"Come and sit back down, Mandi. Wow, you really are thinking about all the big changes. So I'm going to be honest, I'd already thought about talking to you about what we'd do when your week here was over. I don't want to lose this connection with you, and I've really enjoyed getting to know you better, so the idea of you staying on at the Ranch sounds really lovely."

When Mandi smiled, it was one full of hope, and Amelia wanted to never see that fade.

"I do think you're right, and moving into the Littles' Wing is a good idea; but we could date and maybe, later down the line, we could, as you say, u-haul it and move in together, if that's something that you'd like. But like you said, there'd be no rush. Have you spoken to Master Derek yet?"

"No, not yet. I wanted to speak to you first and see if you'd be comfortable with it. Because, you see, I was hoping that I might be able to stay on as an assistant librarian. I've really enjoyed working with you, and there are so many things from my undergrad course I could bring into the library, but I didn't know if you'd feel comfortable with me staying in that role, especially if we continue… well… you know."

Amelia did indeed know. "I see," she said, "well I wouldn't have any concerns about you staying in that role. We've been considering advertising the post anyway, so it's not like we'd be creating the job for you exactly. And I would certainly support your application. I've seen how much you love your job, you're really good at it, and the way you've worked with the other Littles has been fantastic. You'd be an asset to the staff."

Mandi looked excited. "Do you think… do you think I should speak to Master Derek then? About the possibility of staying?"

"Yes," said Amelia, her heart full. "I really, really do."

CHAPTER 24

BOOKING an appointment to see Master Derek was far more intimidating than just bouncing into his office with Sadie. Mandi had messaged Sadie in the morning, and Sadie pointed her in the direction of Erika.

Erika was lovely, super friendly and smiley, and managed to slip her in to see Master Derek almost immediately.

"Hey there, little lady," said Master Derek as she walked in. "And how are you doing?"

"If it's okay," said Mandi taking a seat, timid but determined, "this is a meeting I'd rather not be in Little space for, please, so if you could just call me Mandi, that would make it easier for me."

He sat up in his chair, "Of course, Mandi. Is everything okay? If anything untoward has happened—"

"Oh no," she quickly reassured him, "it's just that this is more of a Big conversation than a Little one, and I don't want you to think it's just a whim."

"I see," he leaned back in his chair. "Lay it on me."

"I've been thinking and I was wondering if I could move onto the Ranch, on a trial period. I know you have a number of Littles and submissives who live on site, and I was wondering if I could be one of them. I wouldn't want to enroll in the Little school, or the university though; I would like to work here—mainly in Big mode—as the assistant librarian in the Littles' Library, but then live here as a Little."

Master Derek didn't say anything. She waited, fidgeting a little, brushing her toes back and forth over the tassels on the edge of the office's rug.

"Is it because of Amelia Grayson?"

"No," she said. "I've discussed it with her, of course, as she'd be my direct line manager if the assistant librarian job was suitable; and also because we would like to continue getting to know each other. Dating. But I'd be asking this even if she wasn't in the picture." She leaned forward. "You've created a space that's safe for Littles and submissives specifically, but I don't think you realize how safe it is for neurodiverse people like myself. The world isn't always kind to us, and I've made myself smaller for so long. But here? Here I feel free to be myself, however scary a concept that may be."

"I'm glad you've found it helpful, but it isn't an easy decision to make, and certainly not a small one."

"That's why I thought a trial might be a good idea; maybe a month. See how it works, whether it works, and then decide after that whether I'm a good fit for the Ranch, and whether the Ranch is a good fit for me."

"That seems very sensible," said Master Derek. "You've really thought this all through."

"Uh huh, and I talked to my cousin about it." Mandi leaned back, pulling her legs up beneath her until she was fully ensconced on three sides by the large armchair. "I need something to change, I need to live the life I've always dreamed of, and I've struggled to do it out there, in a world that is actively hostile toward me. I'd really like to explore the possibility of living somewhere that won't make it harder to simply live my life."

"Would you be open to sharing a room?"

Mandi thought about it. "Maybe for the trial, and then see how that goes? Sometimes, if I'm very overwhelmed, I can't cope with talking to other people. But I wouldn't want special treatment."

"That's okay," said Master Derek, "I think I know exactly the right person to share with you. And we can look into what job would suit you best; it might be the assistant librarian, and it might be that something else would suit you better, though I somehow doubt it. I really am glad you feel so comfortable here, but I'd like to encourage you, the last few days of this week, to try and spend some time with some of the Littles you haven't met yet. I know it's a bit overwhelming, but I feel like it would really help you see if you'd feel comfortable living here."

"Okay," said Mandi, putting her determined face on. "I'll have lunch with some of the other Littles today. I can do it!"

"How about I call down Tay now, and the two of you can go together?" asked Derek. "I think the two of you would really get on."

"Okay," said Mandi and waited nervously to meet her potential roommate.

Tay was cheerful, calm and nonbinary. "They/them pronouns," they announced after Master Derek had introduced them, and they and Mandi headed down to the cafeteria together.

"She/her," replied Mandi. "Have you been staying here long?"

Tay grinned, "Yeah, I've been here for nearly a year. I work over in the Italian restaurant; make fresh pasta every day and feast like royalty! So Master Derek said you might be my roomie?"

Mandi nodded. "That's right; I'm considering moving here permanently, and Master Derek agreed that a trial period might be a good idea first." She paused, suddenly hungry. "Where do you want to eat?"

"Well, I've been given lunch off to show you around, so let's go to the Italian restaurant, I can show you my domain! You like pasta?"

Mandi nodded. "It's delicious."

"Just wait til you try mine!"

She could see why Master Derek had picked Tay as a prospective roommate. They were friendly but not too overwhelmingly chatty, and also seemed to have a Big job that they did by day. "And you're a Little… one?"

"Little one, that's right; it's the ideal pet name for an enby like me."

"And do you have a Caregiver?"

Tay's face didn't fall exactly, but there was certainly a feeling there that Mandi guessed might feel like sadness. "Nah, I'm fine without a Dom—all they do is boss us around and I'm not the biggest fan of that. Makes living under Nanny J's watchful eye interesting though."

"I bet! So how do you balance it; the Big job and the Little living?"

They went to slip their arm through Mandi's and paused. "I'm sorry, my bad, you okay if we link arms?"

"Sure!" She really didn't mind at all, but she also liked that Tay had asked.

They linked up, and then headed on into the restaurant together. "So it's a bit strange really; most of the Littles and Middles here are in that headspace all the time, but there are a couple of us who slip in and out. It's not exactly the same as switching but allows me that same versatility. I don't like being tied down to one thing." They grinned at Mandi. "My gender presentation makes a whole load of sense now, right?"

Tay had a bit of a mullet, with a short, buzzed undercut beneath the longer sections of their hair, and married it with jeans and a lacy jumper dress. It felt very them.

"Never liked being shoved in a box."

"I get that," said Mandi. "Not from a gender-identity perspective, but definitely as a neurodiverse person."

"You're neurospicy too? Well, doesn't that just feel like it was meant to be."

"Neurospicy?" Mandi laughed. "I'd never considered it like that before. I like that."

"It's 'cause we're spicy as anything, and too much for most people to handle."

The words "too much" hit her hard, but then she realized that Tay had used it to describe themself. It hadn't been an insult, or something negative. Mandi hadn't ever heard anyone use it like that before, and it made her wonder if she'd ever be able to use those words like that herself.

"Too much spice is never a bad thing," said Tay, with a teasing nudge. "We're just an acquired taste."

CHAPTER 25

Lunch with Tay was a lot of fun. The Italian restaurant had been really noisy, but Mandi had popped in her engage earplugs, so that she could still chat to her new friend and still lessen the noise of the rest of the clientele.

And then, after lunch, Tay took her back into the kitchen to meet the rest of the chefs, including Chef Guilia, whose stern façade took in the two giggling Littles, and set them up with homemade ice cream on a table in the corner of the kitchen.

"You behaving, Tay?"

"Yes, Chef," said Tay cheerfully, adding to Mandi under their breath, "at least, as far as they're concerned."

They managed to sneak some extra ice cream, got a disapproving look sent their way when they were chattering too noisily, and then escaped out onto the wraparound porch before the missing ice cream could be discovered.

They sat on one of the porch swings together and gently rocked back and forth—though not so fast or so high that Mandi could tumble off again.

"What do you like about being here?" she asked.

"It's the fact that I can be myself," explained Tay. "I don't have to pretend to be cis; I don't have to pretend to be neurotypical. I can just be. And sure, there are punishments if you break a rule, or pull a prank, but that's okay, I don't mind that. If anything, it's nice to know that someone cares enough to notice. But being me... that's not a luxury given to many of us in the world outside Rawhide."

"No," agreed Mandi.

"How about you? Why are you thinking of moving here?"

"Pretty much the same as you; I don't have to pretend. I'm tired of pretending to be someone I'm not, and I'd really rather like to be done with that sort of thing. But outside the Ranch, you can't." Even thinking about it made Mandi feel something akin to grief, grief for the life she could have had, if there world was just a tad bit kinder to people like her and Tay.

"No," said Tay sadly. "Sometimes you really can't. Master Derek and his staff at Rawhide have created a haven for people like us; people who need shelter from the storm that is our life. And then we get to build a new one while we're here."

"That sounds like the reason I moved here too," said a familiar voice.

"Mommy Amelia!" said Mandi. "Come meet Tay!"

"Hey, Tay," said Mommy Amelia.

"Hi, Miss Grayson," said Tay. "So *you're* the reason Mandi here is so keen to stay."

"No! That's not... I didn't... *Tay*..." said Mandi, completely flustered.

Tay laughed. "I'm only teasing. Working with your Mommy Domme though... That's certainly an interesting prospect." They looked thoughtful and Mandi wondered if there was more between Tay and Chef Guilia than just ice cream.

"May I pull up a chair?" asked Mommy Amelia, and Mandi and Tay happily acquiesced. "Master Derek said you two might be sharing a room together."

The two of them shared a look, neither one wanting to be the first to talk. Eventually, Mandi bit the bullet and spoke, "Well, we get on pretty well, and I think that if I'm going to share a room with someone, them being neurodiverse—neuro*spicy*—can only help. It means we won't need to explain *all* of our reasoning to each other. Sometimes we'll just get it."

Tay nodded. "And I'll be happier sharing with someone who's queer for exactly the same reason. There are some things we just don't need to explain."

"Queer shorthand," said Mommy Amelia. "Makes perfect sense to me; I know it well. And you manage to balance the Big and Little sides of your life okay?"

"Yeah, at work I'm Pastaio Tay, just another person in the kitchen; and when I'm done for the day, I'm just Tay, chaotic Little one with a penchant for ice cream and mischief." They shot a look at Mommy Amelia. "Not that I'll be getting Mandi into trouble; that's not my style."

Mommy Amelia chuckled. "We'll see; I have a feeling that my Little has mischievousness of her own tucked up her sleeves."

Mandi made a big production of looking up both her sleeves. "Nope, Mommy, no mischievousness here!"

"It'll be nice," Tay added, "to have someone else who's not Little all the time on the Littles' Wing. Sometimes it can get a bit lonely if everyone else is so Little that I can't offload about my day to them."

"I can see that," said Mandi. She smiled. "I think we'd

make good roommates, if you're not too sad about no longer having the room to yourself."

"I've been hoping for a roomie for some time," said Tay. "Here's to new beginnings!"

CHAPTER 26

"I WAS WONDERING if you'd like to have dinner at my house tonight," said Amelia, when they had both said goodbye to Tay and walked back over to the Littles' Library. "We have to go through the tunnels, and then take one of the golf carts, but if you're up for it, I'd love to show you my home."

Amelia was trying very hard not to make a big deal out of this proposition, when in fact it was a big deal. A huge one.

Ever since she'd moved into her house on Rawhide Ridge, she'd never had someone come and stay. Not even visit for dinner. She might have made an off the cuff comment a few days ago about doing a scene there, but it hadn't meant that she'd actually been ready to do such a thing.

Now though, now she wanted to show Mandi her home, small though it was.

"I'd love that!" Mandi said, eyes shining. "And maybe we could cook together?"

"I've actually got something prepared; if you like curry, that is?"

Mandi clapped her hands in delight. "Yes, yes, *yes*. That

sounds delicious! Head over straight after the library closes?"

"Indeed."

The next four hours dragged by. Amelia was tempted to get up and go see what Mandi was doing almost every other moment. But she had her own work to do and set about updating the system with new books that had recently arrived, scanning them, and placing them on the trolley, ready for shelving.

Next she supervised a relatively rowdy game of Monopoly, keeping a close eye on a fairly mutinous-looking Sadie, who lost in spectacular fashion, and finished off the afternoon with straightening up.

She didn't usually finish until seven, but Derek had adjusted the library hours this week, to take into account the fact that had Mandi in her charge, but she knew it wouldn't last when Mandi moved onto the Ranch permanently. She'd already talked it through with Derek. She'd still open at nine in the morning, but finish earlier, around five; and Mandi would start at eleven and stay until closing, including at seven on the library's late opening days when it was usually quieter anyway. That way she'd be able to cook dinner for her Little girl each evening. And they'd both get Sundays off, and if people wanted to order books, games or art supplies, they'd do what they did now, which was to order them via room service. The concierge team knew where everything was, and if something seemed to be missing, they'd email her and she'd deal with it on Monday.

It was a sound plan of action, and one that not only gave her more time off in the evenings but had built into it the fact she was starting to want to do something outside of work.

Something?

Make that some*one*.

But all jokes aside, she really did value the time she got with Mandi, and she wanted the evening to reflect that.

She sent Mandi off to pack an overnight bag—just in case—and waited for her patiently by the elevators.

Amelia felt surprisingly nervous. Her home was small, but it was hers. She'd decorated it simply, with wooden furniture and small pieces of art, and she hoped beyond hope that Mandi liked it.

Mandi certainly liked the golf cart ride, making silly zoom-y noises happily the whole ride, and then when they arrived outside Amelia's home, Amelia could tell by her happy wiggles that she liked that too.

It was a simple house, in the log-cabin style, with a small, fenced garden out the back, and lawn with flowers in the front.

"Oh," Mandi breathed. "Isn't it pretty!"

Hiding her pleasure behind gruffness, Amelia said, "Yeah, it's okay."

"Mommy! It's not just okay, look at your *flowers*! You have daisies everywhere."

Usually, Amelia cursed the darn daisies that seemed to overtake every square inch of her front lawn, but Mandi was so enchanted by them that she forgave them immediately.

Opening the front door, Mandi was instantly entranced by the ladder that led to the loft.

"What's up there, Mommy?" she asked.

"Oh, that's where I sleep."

Wide-eyed, Mandi went for the ladder first and, head and shoulders disappearing, called down, "You can see the stars!"

"That was the idea," said Amelia. It had actually been the detail that had sold her on the house in the first place. She really did need to take Derek up on his offer to sell it to her, instead of just renting it to her. "Would you like the grand tour?"

There were only a few rooms: a kitchen, looking as rustic as ever a kitchen looked, but with excellent appliances, including a dishwasher, because Amelia hated washing dishes; a bathroom with bath and shower, though not as grandiose as the one in Mandi's suite; a second bedroom, which Amelia used as a backup study; and the living room, which was where she spent most of her time.

There was a fireplace, which she set to lighting as they walked in. "Why don't you settle on the couch there, petal, and warm yourself under a blanket, while I get this fire going. And then I can get dinner on."

Mandi nodded, looking around. "It's really cozy, Mommy. I like all the autumnal colors."

"I'm glad, babygirl," she said. She'd designed it for herself, never expecting to find the Little of her dreams, but now that she had, she was glad Mandi loved her home too. It bode well for their possible future.

Dinner was quite satisfactory, although from the noises Mandi made while eating, anyone would've thought that Amelia had cooked up an entire banquet for the two of them.

"What would you like to do now, babygirl?" asked Amelia, when the dishes had been cleared away, and everything was quiet.

"I'd like for you to make love to me," said Mandi, her shy frankness endearing. "If that's okay?"

"Here?"

"Here," she said. "Make love to me by the fire."

CHAPTER 27

Mandi didn't know what had come over her, but whatever it was, she liked it. She liked this bolder side of herself who wasn't scared of so many things.

Maybe it was Mommy Amelia, maybe it was Rawhide Ranch, maybe it was just herself. No matter what, she determined that this attitude was here to stay.

It was invigorating.

She stood, emboldened by the desire in Mommy Amelia's eyes, and in the flickering light of the fireplace, Mandi started to undress.

She'd never done something like this before, but the way Mommy Amelia's gaze followed her, hungry for each inch that was revealed… well, it was everything. She could feel the excitement thrumming through her veins, threatening to send her off-kilter, dizzily into Mommy's arms, but still Mandi continued on.

Her top was discarded first, then her trousers, and then the cute frilly bra and panties set that she had on beneath, until nothing but the flamelight touched her skin.

Mommy slipped off the couch and crawled on her

knees toward Mandi. "My darling, beautiful girl. Look at you."

And Mandi did. She looked down and fully luxuriated in all the softness of her curves, the fullness of her hips and belly and tush. Breasts that moved heavily, skin that dimpled when touched, and touch it Mommy Amelia did.

She took Mandi by the tush and pulled her close until Mommy Amelia's nose was nudging at Mandi's curls.

"Open your legs for me, princess, and let me take a walk inside your garden."

Trembling, ever so slightly, Mandi shuffled her feet apart and then moaned when Mommy Amelia parted her curls with her fingers, stroking her own slick desire up a path to her clit.

She could feel it, throbbing, wanting to be touched, wanting to be stroked and coaxed forward into the pleasure of a warm mouth, but instead Mommy Amelia danced around it, gently blowing until Mandi wanted to scream in frustration.

"Please, Mommy, I need you to touch me."

"But I am touching you, princess." A single finger traced her outside lips. "See? Touching."

"But... but... not there!"

"Not there? You want me to touch you somewhere else?"

"You know where I want you to touch me!"

"Now, now," said Mommy Amelia, "I seem to remember *someone* telling me to use *my* words. I think turnabout is fair play, especially for someone who so brazenly and beautifully stripped for me in front of this fire."

Mandi flushed. Using her words was hard, harder than stripping for her Mommy, but she could do it. "Please, can you touch my clit, Mommy?"

One thumb came to rest atop her clit.

She looked down, past her softness, to where Mommy Amelia's face was resting on her belly, looking up at her. "I'm going to have to spell it out, aren't I, Mommy?"

"In excruciating detail, my dear."

Mandi took a deep breath. "Please, Mommy, I want to feel your fingers teasing my clit, and then your tongue, and then your mouth. I want to feel good, the way only you can make me feel. I want to come apart for you, because I know you'll help me piece the pieces back together. I want to come for you, Mommy, to show you how much I trust you with myself."

And then all her words were stolen because Mommy Amelia had buried her face in Mandi's cunt, and was licking and teasing and sucking, almost all at once—if such a thing was even possible.

She brought Mandi to the edge, over and over, never once letting her crest the wave. Instead, she'd pull back each time, until Mandi begged her for more, begged and pleaded and keened for her climax.

"Come, darling," Mommy Amelia said, urging Mandi down into her lap, "sit here and feel good."

Without urging, Mandi found herself riding Mommy Amelia's hand, rising up and then lowering herself onto fingers that made her feel impossibly full.

"You're going to ride my hand, sweet girl, while I play with your clit. And when I decide it's time, when I know you cannot take anymore, I'm going to take you there. Yes?"

"Yes, Mommy," she gasped out, her head falling backward as she rode more and more vigorously. "Please, Mommy."

"It's okay, darling," guided Mommy Amelia. "I know you can take more, I know you can hold out for me, wait for me until I'm ready to let you come."

Every cell was desperate for release, her entire body

taut with longing. Held there, quivering, waiting, waiting until Mommy Amelia kissed her fiercely and then whispered in her ear, "Come for me, princess, come for the Mommy who loves you."

And Mandi came.

CHAPTER 28

THE CABIN WAS super quiet to sleep in. The window above Mommy Amelia's bed showed a canopy of stars above them, all bright and shining for the two of them.

They snuggled up close together, pajamas cast aside in favor of skin touching skin. As Mommy Amelia slept, Mandi lay awake for a while, looking up at the heavens.

Hey, universe, she thought. *It's been a whole while but look at me now.*

The last time she'd lain in bed like this, thinking thoughts out into the ether, it had been after her breakup and she'd lain frozen, numb, lost.

Now though, she felt alive, warm... found. She'd found herself again, found her Little, found her home. She was taking life and making it her bitch. Well, maybe not quite that, but something approximating that.

She was going to have a roommate, which was exciting! And it seemed like she and Tay were going to become friends. That was good; she definitely needed more friends.

Mandi vowed then and there to speak to at least one new person every day—outside of her job. It didn't have to be a long conversation, but a few sentences exchanged, and soon she'd find herself with lots of new friends, and perhaps slightly less scared of meeting strangers.

Mommy Amelia snuffled and rolled over, and Mandi giggled. She really was the luckiest with her Mommy. She was kind and funny and hotter than hell itself. And she was going to explore this *thing* they had between them, let it play out slowly, like a proper relationship. Put down roots, grounding so they didn't become unmoored in every storm that passed them.

Mandi smiled and nestled up against Mommy Amelia to sleep.

When she awoke, blinking, in dawn's sweet colors, Mommy Amelia was still fast asleep. Quietly, she snuck out of bed and managed to make her way down the ladder without bumping her head.

Tiptoeing across the cabin, she made it to her bag and extricated the card and pens she hidden in there.

It was Mother's Day and she was going to make sure that her Mommy had the best card the world had ever seen.

It was safe to say that Mandi was not an artist.

She'd tried, that much was clear, but apparently she could not draw flowers. She'd abandoned the flower idea in favor of drawing bookcases briefly but abandoned it when it became apparent they just looked like the world's largest ladder. So flowers it was.

Her roses looked droopy, her daisies chaotic, and the grass looked like tiny green knives, stabbing upwards.

But inside, inside she'd managed to redeem herself.

Dear Mommy,

. . .

Before I met you, I didn't really know what it was that I was looking for in a partner, I didn't really think that I even wanted one, but somehow you came into my life and I instantly felt safe.

You feel solid, like someone I can lean on when I'm anxious, but also when I'm happily sleepy after a nice day.

Spending time together and getting to know you has made me understand the kind of person I want to be and helped me realize some of those goals. Every day I strive to be more confident, open to meeting new people, and adventurous; because without adopting those three qualities, even for a moment, I'd never have met you.

I love you.

Your,
   Mandi

She popped it onto a tray she found in the kitchen, along with a mug of coffee and a plate of Italian pastries she and Tay had begged from Chef Guilia, and managed—somehow—to balance it as she made it back up the ladder.

A very sleepy Mommy Amelia sat up at the sound of her tripping over the top rung and swearing softly. "Is that my sweary princess?"

"Yes, sorry, Mommy! I almost spilt your coffee."

"Coffee, oh you angel, let me look at—" When the other woman turned her sleepy gaze on Mandi, her mouth dropped open in surprise. "Is that… are those… pastries?"

"It's Mothers' Day," explained Mandi. "I know you're not really, but you're *my* Mommy and so it only seemed fair that you get breakfast in bed, and a card. I drew it myself," she added sheepishly.

But to be fair to Mommy Amelia, she didn't laugh at the card, not even at Mandi's attempt at drawing a tiny ant, that looked more like a felled body than an insect. "You made this for me?" she said, and then went very quiet indeed as she read the message on the inside.

Mandi stood awkwardly, waiting for the verdict, and then fell upon the bed to kiss her Mommy when Mommy Amelia turned eyes brimming with tears upon her.

"No, no, no, Mommy!" she said, covering her face with kisses. "No tears; it's 'cause I love you."

"I love you too, my darling, and I can't wait to show you all the ways in which I do. You"—Mommy Amelia paused, taking in a jagged breath—"have changed my life completely, babygirl. I was content, but you've brought joy. Laughter. Things that always felt like they belonged to other people and not me." Tears fell now, not sad tears, Mandi realized, but happy tears. "I'm happy, petal, and I don't think I knew that I wasn't happy before."

"We shall be happy together," said Mandi.

"Yes," said Mommy Amelia, brown eyes shining, and Mandi determined to always bring her Mommy happiness.

"Happy Mother's Day, Mommy," she said, and kissed her love.

EPILOGUE

One Month Later

Mandi snatched her lunch bag from the counter where Tay had placed it and shouted her thanks over her shoulder. Sometimes she came and ate in the Italian restaurant with her new friends, but often she grabbed the lunch her roomie made her and went and sat outside to eat on one of the porch swings.

Today was one of those days.

It was a Sunday, a full four weeks since Mother's Day and since Mandi had confirmed with Master Derek that she wanted to move onto the Ranch.

She wove in and out, making her way between chattering Littles, until she found her favorite swing free. Someone—Mommy Amelia—had placed Beau there, with a jaunty sign that read *Reserved for Miss Mandi*.

That's what the other Littles called her when she was in librarian mode, Miss Mandi, with a cheeky smile that usually indicated that they saw her more as a big sister or aunty than one of the "proper" Bigs. And that suited Mandi fine. She was perfectly content to be a friendly face, rather than one associated with discipline. Though she had been known to have stern words with some of the Butterflies when they started throwing books around.

But she felt more settled than she'd ever been before.

Sharing a room with Tay had been the most fun. They had similar working hours, and it meant that if Mandi wasn't staying at Mommy Amelia's house, then they got to hang out together after work, have Little time, and chatter away.

They were both the anomalies in the Littles' Wing, having Big jobs that took up most of their week, but Master Derek had allowed them a smidgeon more freedom than he did the other Littles, and they were determined not to take advantage of it and lose privileges.

Tay was a naughty Little though and could often be found sneaking treats out of the kitchens, and Mandi had adjusted to the fact that what appeared to be a mini-freezer permanently full of Chef Guilia's homemade ice cream lived in a corner of their room.

She'd made friends, spent more time than Mandi had ever dared before in Little Space, and had loveliest Mommy-princess dates every week.

She sat on the porch swing, opened her lunchbox, and smiled at the note that Mommy Amelia had managed to smuggle in. Mandi never caught her handing it over to Tay, but there it was every day, folded in increasingly pretty origami patterns in her lunchbox.

Usually they'd spend Sunday together, but Master Derek had recommended that Mandi take some time on her own today, to really think about how she'd adjusted to living on the Ranch full-time.

"It's no small decision, little lady," he'd said. "And I don't want you making the wrong one and regretting it."

"Mandi!" She looked up, and to her surprise saw her

cousin running as fast as he could up the very long drive to the main house.

"Ralphie?" What was he doing here?

Ever since she'd started her trial stay, the two of them had called weekly, catching up on what was going on each other's lives, and she'd come to value those phone calls, the only ones she really had from the outside world.

He paused his running to catch his breath and waved wildly at her. Behind him was a very bemused Nate, his fiancé, who was taking his time strolling up the driveway instead of attempting to sprint it.

"How do people make it up here?" asked Ralphie, panting as he dragged himself up the steps of the porch and threw himself onto the swing, next to Mandi. "The drive goes on forever!"

"Usually people get dropped off at the front door," said Mandi.

"Told you so," said Nate, standing the two suitcases he'd been dragging behind him upward.

"And I told *you*, Daddy, that the walk would do us good."

"And did it?"

Ralphie waved his hand dismissively. "Well, I didn't walk it, did I? I ran it, so it's not the correct kind of data."

Nate huffed out a laugh and smiled at Mandi. "Hey, Mandi, apologies for just turning up. *Someone* wanted to surprise you."

"The someone was me!" said Ralphie loftily. "'Cause today's the end of your first month, right? I wanted to be here so that you've got someone impartial to talk to." He turned to Nate. "You may take the bags in, Daddy. Mandi and I have much to discuss."

Nate bared his teeth at Mandi's cousin and growled. Ralphie, rather than being intimidated by this, merely grinned and said, "Later, Daddy, later."

His fiancé rolled his eyes, leaned over to kiss him, and then took the suitcases indoors, leaving the two cousins on the swing together.

She hugged him impulsively. "You came!"

"Of course," said Ralphie, looking confused. "Shouldn't I have?"

"No no," said Mandi. "I'm so so pleased to see you, I just didn't expect—" Her voice trailed off, and she hugged him harder.

"We're better than family," said Ralphie. "We're the family that we chose. And that means I'm always going to be in your life. And that I'm going to pop up out of nowhere to surprise you when you've got big things going on."

She nodded. "Thank you."

"Of course," said Ralphie. "Now, the exciting bit. What've you decided?"

Mandi's eyes brimmed with tears, and she smiled shakily. "I'm staying, I think."

"You think?"

"I'm staying." Her voice still sounded shaky though, and Ralphie dropped his chaotic energy by at least half, and looked at her worriedly.

"Talk to me, 'coz."

"I love it here," she said. "I've made incredible friends—wait til you meet Tay, you'll love them—Mommy Amelia is incredible, my job is great, it's just…"

"Yes?"

"It's a big decision. And what if I regret it later?"

"It's not a cult, Mandi, you can leave at any time. I mean, you can, right?"

She nodded. "I can, I just don't want to rush into selling my duplex, there's not enough room for all my things in my room here…"

"You can rent the duplex out, and if there's stuff you

need to put in storage, there's space at Stuffie Hospital. I got you. I don't want you not to do this because you're afraid it might go wrong. Anything can go wrong, but this time, you're not on your own. You have me and Nate, you have Mommy Amelia and Master Derek, you have Tay and Sadie and all the other friends you've made here. None of that has to disappear if you end up changing your mind."

Mandi nodded, and hugged Beau to her, leaning back to let the porch swing rock gently. That had been the thing she'd been dwelling on the last few days, the finality of it all if she sold her duplex. Right now it was there, a cushion if she fell, but if it was taken away from her…

"But doesn't it seem like I don't think this will work out if I don't sell the duplex?"

Ralphie looked confused. "Not really, it just seems like a smart business investment, in case you—or you and Mommy Amelia—decide to buy a place yourselves, further down the line. It can sit there, paying its own mortgage, and all you have to do is collect rent. I'll even be your general handyman for the place if you like."

"How about *I* do the handyman work," interjected Nate as he rejoined them. "I'm rather sure she'd like the work to be done both quickly and efficiently."

"Well!" Ralphie drew himself up to his full height. "I must say. The *slander*."

Mandi laughed, "That sounds lovely; thank you, guys."

"You're welcome."

"What's all this then?" asked a warm voice behind them. Mandi swiveled on the swing to see her Mommy striding toward them.

"Mommy!" she called, "It's my cousin Ralphie, and his fiancé Nate! They've come to visit."

"Hi there," said Mommy Amelia, extending her hand for Nate and then Ralphie to shake. "I'm ever so grateful to you both for persuading her to come visit; and I won't be sad to say that we've stolen her away somewhat."

"That's okay," said Ralphie. "She's delectable, I understand why you'd want her to stay."

Mandi shook her head and laughed.

"And she'll be even more delectable in a bridesmaid's dress—you *will* be a groomsmaid at our wedding, won't you?" Ralphie took both her hands in his and pleaded.

"A groomsmaid? Me?"

"*Please!* You won't even have to do any of the organizing, I'm already making one of my other groomsmaids do all the boring bits. I…" Ralphie's voice trailed off. "You're the family I've chosen for myself, and we both know that the rest of our relatives—I'm not even sure if my sister will agree to come. But we talk, and kinda gossip—though I do more gossiping than you do—and you give good advice and you're sweet, and you'll look *divine* in green velvet, with all that red hair. Please?"

"Of course I will," she said, and hugged him. "I would love that."

"And you'll come too, Amelia?" asked Nate.

Ralphie spun around. "Oh shit, yes, you too!"

The head librarian laughed. "I'd love to, thank you."

With that settled, Nate dragged Ralphie off to their room, to try and calm him down, he said; though Mandi couldn't even comprehend such a scenario.

Mommy Amelia came and sat on the swing next to her, slipping her arm around Mandi's shoulder. "I bet this was the perfect thinking spot before that."

"It still is," she said, and kissed her Mommy on the cheek.

"And?"

"And I'm staying." She didn't elaborate and could feel Amelia's eyes watching her. "Okay, look. I love you, and I love life here on the Ranch, but I don't want to sell my duplex just yet. I think I'm going to rent it out, pay off some more of the mortgage, and then when maybe we want to move in together, I can sell it and use that as a down payment somewhere."

Mommy Amelia stopped the swing from rocking with her foot. "You don't like my place?"

Mandi felt that rising panic and squashed it down. Nope. This wasn't a scary conversation, she didn't need to panic. "I love your place, but if we're going to move in together, then I'd like to be on the deed. I know you've been talking to Master Derek about buying it, and that's a brilliant plan, but I want the option of being a part of that."

Her Mommy nodded, and Mandi allowed the tension in her body to dissipate slowly. "I just need a safety net. Not forever, but for now."

"My darling," said Mommy Amelia, leaning in to kiss her, "You get to have whatever you need to be safe. There's no rush here. I'm not going anywhere."

"And neither am I," said Mandi, and kissed her back.

***

That afternoon, Mandi got called down to Master Derek's office, and she almost skipped in, considering how different her life was now from what it had been a mere month previous.

"Hi, Master Derek," she said, and clambered onto one of the large armchairs and made herself comfy.

He looked bemused and a little proud at her confidence. "Well, isn't this a nice change from the first time we met?"

Mandi smiled. She felt like she couldn't be further from the terrified woman who'd sobbed on the couch before. It wasn't that she was fixed, trauma didn't work like that, but she was working on herself and had tools and a support network that had simply not been there before. "Yeah, who could have guessed that we'd be having this conversation back then?"

"So."

"So."

"Have you made up your mind?"

"I have," she said. "I'd like to stay. I'm going to keep my old duplex for now and rent it out so I can keep paying the mortgage."

"Have you thought about where you'd like to live?"

She nodded decisively. "Yes, Tay and I spoke about it and we'd like to keep on as we are for now. They're a great roomie, and we understand each other."

"And Miss Grayson?"

Mandi melted, the way she did whenever anyone mentioned Mommy Amelia. "We're going to keep dating, with me spending the night at her house regularly. There's no rush to move in together straight away, and actually I think it'll be good for me to foster some independence." She smiled. "It's funny; so many of us Littles come here, looking to build a relationship where they don't have to make decisions anymore, whereas I think I actually still need that autonomy sometimes. That way when I do as I'm told, I know I'm doing it because I've chosen to, and not because I've fallen back into bad habits."

"It sounds like you've been doing a lot of growing, this last month." Master Derek sounded impressed. "I'm really proud of you, you know. It can't have been easy, forcing yourself out of your comfort zone."

"And yet it brought me to this moment, where I've never been more comfortable. I can't take all the credit though," she added. "Cat Denten is an incredible psychologist and getting to keep on working with her is definitely a big factor in me staying. You look after your own, and that makes Rawhide Ranch special."

"I couldn't have put it better myself," said Master Derek. "Now, the last thing I wanted to ask about was a problem we're having in one of the kitchens. Chef Guilia has been complaining about ice cream going missing; I know that you're in and out of there regularly, with Tay. Do you know anything about it?"

Mandi chose her words carefully. "I've not been involved in the liberation of any ice cream," she answered, her words deliberately not directly answering the question. She wasn't going to get Tay into trouble, although she rather thought that Tay was looking forward to getting caught. "Maybe there's a mouse who's fond of dairy on the loose?"

That might have been pushing it a tad too far. Master Derek raised an eyebrow and Mandi squirmed in her seat.

"Perhaps. I don't suppose you could ask Tay to come and see me? In case they could shed some light on the matter?"

Mandi nodded and made her escape.

But outside the door to the office, she found a veritable crowd of people waiting for her: Mommy Amelia, Tay, Sadie, Chef Guilia, Miss Price, Nanny J, and even Ralphie and Nate.

"Well?" asked Sadie, clearly too impatient to wait another second. "What did he say?"

"I can stay," she said, and Mandi was almost swept off her feet with all the hugs and excitement and well-wishes. Over Sadie and Tay's heads, she caught Ralphie's eye. Her cousin nodded, clearly satisfied with the outcome.

"Right," said Mommy Amelia, "I'm stealing my girl off for the rest of the day; I've had to share her with everyone else all morning."

Mandi laughed at the complaints, but followed Mommy Amelia when the other woman took her hand and led her out the front door and down the main steps to where a golf cart was waiting.

"Are we off to your place?" Mandi asked, but instead of turning right and heading toward Rawhide Ridge, they turned left, toward the Big House.

Mommy Amelia parked before they got there though, and took Mandi by the hand, and started heading across the grass toward a large lake.

"I've never been here before," said Mandi, looking out across the expanse of water.

"It's one of my favorite places to come in the summer," said her Mommy. "Come on."

There was a little row boat tied up to the dock, a picnic basket nestled up in the bow. Mommy Amelia jumped in, and then handed Mandi in carefully.

"You sit there, princess, and I'll row."

"Okay," Mandi said happily, and took her seat without complaint. There were multiple canoes tied up, but no one else was anywhere to be seen. "Can anyone come here?"

"Well, Littles need permission, obviously, but it's available for swimming and all sorts. I asked Master Derek if we could have it to ourselves this afternoon."

She rowed across the lake with strong strokes, her jacket discarded, and her sleeves rolled up. Mandi took the opportunity to watch her, reveling in the forearms on display, and chuckled happily to herself.

Late afternoon, and it was cool in the shady spot on the bank that Mommy Amelia tied the boat to. She didn't let Mandi do anything, laying out the picnic blanket and then extra cushions and blankets, so that Mandi could snuggle up. Beau had a cushion all his own to sit on.

The picnic basket itself was stuffed full of all kinds of goodies. Small pastries, a salad, and a whole array of different fruits including strawberries—Mandi's favorite.

"This is incredible, Mommy," she said. "What's all this for?"

"I just wanted to show you," said Mommy Amelia, "how excited I am that you're staying. We'd have made it work either way, but I can't wait to explore the Ranch with you. To show you my favorite spots—just like this one—and for us to make new memories. Seeing you blossom this last month, watching you make new friends and come into your own has been beautiful." She leaned forward and tucked Mandi's hair behind her ear. "I'm never going to take you for granted, babygirl. I never expected to find you, and now that I have, I'm going to cherish every moment we spend together."

Mandi looked up at the leafy canopy above them and closed her eyes, breathing in the quiet around them. "I'm home," she said. Opening her eyes, she pressed a kiss to her Mommy's cheek. "Home and safe with you. I love you, Mommy."

"I love you too, babygirl," said Mommy Amelia. "Now and always."

THE END

You are Invited to Ralphie and Nate's Wedding!

A Little's Christmas Wedding

A Stuffie Hospital Age Play Romance

Ellie Rose

It's Ralphie Underwood's wedding day to Nate Pace, but when a storm ruins their wedding venue, it's Stuffie Hospital to the rescue!

Visit Stuffie Hospital, a fluffy and steamy romance series, where toys get a new lease of life and queer Littles get their very own happy ever afters!

Preorder Now!

ABOUT RAWHIDE RANCH

Looking for more Rawhide Ranch?
Rawhide Ranch Newsletter: https://authoralliebelle.eo.page/rawhideranch
Rawhide Authors Amazon: https://amzn.to/3wlOOTN
Rawhide Ranch Facebook Page:
https://www.facebook.com/RawhideRanchSeries
Rawhide Ranch Facebook Group:
https://www.facebook.com/groups/rawhideranchseries
Rawhide Website: www.rawhideranchseries.com
Rawhide Instagram: https://www.instagram.com/rawhideranchseries
Rawhide TikTok: https://www.tiktok.com/@rawhideranchseries

ABOUT ELLIE ROSE

Ellie Rose is a queer author who writes fluffy and spicy Little romances as Ellie, and steamy paranormals, and erotic short romances as Ali Williams. Her books are kinky, queer and neurodiverse, and always have a Happy Ever After!

When she's not writing, she can invariably be found reading in her own library (she has over 1500 physical books), traipsing around the South Downs with her girlfriend, or cursing the never-ending work associated with her PhD studies in romance, queerness and kink!

Find Ellie here:
Newsletter: https://mailchi.mp/953263eb76fb/ellie-rose-newsletter
Facebook: https://www.facebook.com/profile.php?id=100080480451125
Reader Group: https://www.facebook.com/groups/shenanigansquad
Website: https://www.ellieroseauthor.com/

ALSO BY ELLIE ROSE

STUFFIE HOSPITAL BOOKS

A Little's Unicorn (Lillie and Aiden's book)
A Little's Reindeer (Georgie and Warren's book)
A Little's Lion (Kacie and Dex's book)
A Little's Patchwork Bear (Ralphie and Nate's book)
A Little's Witchy Bear (Rylie and Eve's book)
A Little's Monster (Christie and Dana's book)
A Little's Dino (Archie and Rebecca's book)
A Little's Elephant (Frankie and Grey's book)
A Little's Owl (Darcie and Richard's book)
A Little's Pegasus (Beanie and Abigail's book)
A Little's Christmas Wedding (Ralphie and Nate's Wedding)

STUFFIE HOSPITAL LONDON BOOKS: A LONDON LITTLE'S LLAMA (BILLIE AND MARK'S BOOK)

A London Little's Moo (Tillie and Alex's book)
A London Little's Dragon (Jamie and Marian's book)
A London Little's Giraffe (Mossie and Daniel's book)
A London Little's Penguin (Rubie and Anna's book)
A London Little's Pom Pom (Rosie and Eloise's book)
A London Little's Bunny (Essie and Ben's book)
A London Little's Octopus (Charlie and Leon's book)
A London Little's Tiger (Susie and Briana's book)

GODSTOUCHED UNIVERSE (AS ALI WILLIAMS): FORGED IN FLAMES: A DRAGON SHIFTER ROMANCE

<u>Value in Visions</u>: A Sapphic Psychic Romance
Married in Moonlight: A Sapphic Psychic Wedding

The Apples Hung like Stars: A Sapphic Fae Romance
Their Fruits like Honey: A Sapphic Fae Romance

Chase Me in the Woods: A Sapphic Shifter Romance
Catch Me in the Dark: A Sapphic Samhain Romance

Nix and Tell: A Sapphic Fae Romance
Never Nix Up: A Sapphic Fae Romance
Don't Give a Nix: A Sapphic Fae Romance

EROTIC ROMANCE (AS ALI WILLIAMS): THE SOFTEST KINKSTERS COLLECTION: AN EROTIC ROMANCE COLLECTION

Kink the Halls: A Sleeping with my Ex's Mum, Lesbian Christmas Romance

Printed in Great Britain
by Amazon